Rosaleen Love was born in Sydney, Australia, in 1940, and grew up in sub-tropical Queensland. She now lives in Melbourne, where she teaches the history of science at Swinburne Institute of Technology. She writes on science for the journals *Australian Society* and *The Age Monthly Review*. This is her first collection of stories. She has recently completed a novel.

Rosaleen Love

The Total Devotion Machine
and Other Stories

The Women's Press
sf

First published by The Women's Press Ltd 1989
A member of the Namara Group
34 Great Sutton Street, London EC1V 0DX

The following stories have been published previously: 'The
Laws of Life' in *Westerly 30*, 1985 and *Coast to Coast* ed
Kerryn Goldsworthy, Angus & Robertson 1986; 'Trickster' in
Overland 103, 1986; 'Alexia and Graham Bell' in *Aphelion 5*,
1986-7; 'Power Play' on *Writers' Radio*, Radio 5UV, June
1987; 'No Resting Place' in *Storyteller 1*, 1987; 'The Sea-
Serpent of Sandy Cape' in *Westerly 32*, 1987; 'The Invisible
Woman' in *Writing Women 6*, 1988.

British Library Cataloguing in Publication Data

Love, Rosaleen
 The Total Devotion Machine and Other Stories
 I. Title
 823 [F]

 ISBN 07043-4188-3

Typeset by Boldface Typesetters, London EC1
Printed and bound in Great Britain by
Cox & Wyman Ltd, Reading, Berks

Contents

This book is for Amy

The Total Devotion Machine

Mary Beth left it until the day before she set sail to tell
Wim Morris and Baby about the Total Devotion Machine. 'This time
tomorrow I'll be off, flying the solar wind to Mars,' she said. 'I have
your interests locked deep in my heart, Wim and Baby dear. Your
fathers did say they'd look after you, according to their respective
shared parenting agreements, but you know all about those contracts
– worthless as the paper on which they are no longer printed. And you
know what men are like – they say one thing and mean it, at the time,
but years later, they forget, they find shared parenting all rather time
consuming, and they'd rather go off and do other things, and so I've
brought you this dinky Total Devotion Machine from the AI Child-
Care Services to look after you while I am gone.'

The Total Devotion Machine shimmered faintly with pleasure, and
gave a maternal wave of its ventral proprioceptors.

'Total devotion, that's your birthright,' says Mary Beth. 'I can't
provide it for you just now; I'm off to Mars, which is my right to
develop myself as an autonomous fully rounded human being with
that extra-terrestrial experience so necessary to climb the promotions
ladder these days.

'I'll be back in a year, Wim Morris, by which time you will have
reached the age of reason, and may even be contemplating entering a
shared parenting contract yourself. And Baby dear, by the time I
return you will be walking and talking a treat! I'll miss you both, but
the machine will send me those interactive videos so necessary for my
full development as a mother, and of course by return I'll send you
back some of me, for your full development as children, and as young

adults. So the time will pass quite quickly, and pleasantly, and efficiently for us all.'

So Mary Beth sailed off on the Tricentennial Fleet, and even the fathers came to wave goodbye, which set back their self-improvement schedules at least an hour. Baby's father, Jemmy, checks the machine over. 'Feel the plastic smile, Baby, isn't it just so supple! Can't tell the difference from the real thing!' he glows.

'I can,' says Wim resentfully. 'When it smiles its eyes glow purple.'

'Purple is a restful colour, specially selected by fully trained child psychologists for optimum soothing power,' Jemmy reads from the brochure.

Wim Morris refuses to accept the explanation in the spirit in which it is given. He continues to carp. 'Why do the eyes have to swivel around on stalks on top of its brain box? Even Baby can spot it's not the same as Mother.'

Baby gurgles and tries to pull the eyes out of their sockets. The Total Devotion Machine glows a faint electric green, and Baby stops at once.

'The eyes rotate through 360 degrees, making a 50 per cent improvement on the human mother,' reads Jemmy.

'Look at it this way, Wim. I'm sure your mother feels much more relaxed about parenting, now she's off, up and away. I know I do.' Wim's father, William, is late for his job, but they understand about parental leave for these moments of temporary parting, and he looks at his watch to check that he's providing his biological and social son with a proper share of quality parenting.

'What about me?' asks Wim.

'I'm sure you and the machine will soon be good pals,' William replies. 'After all, you've got Total Devotion, and who can ask for more?' William and Jemmy hug their children, while explaining firmly that they must leave to go about the business of the brave new world, and to help Mary Beth in her contractual repayments to AI Child-Care Pty Ltd.

'I understand how you feel,' the machine comforts Wim.

'Are you programmed for understanding?' asks Wim suspiciously.

'Total and complete empathy,' replies the machine. 'At your service.'

'Mother, Mother, come back! I didn't mean to shout and scream at you last week, I'm sorry!' Wim calls to the skies.

'Your mother understands,' replies the machine, in a slow and relaxed tone of voice, 'at least I'm sure she would understand if she wasn't on the far side of the Moon by now.'

Wim sobs, and the machine consoles. Baby's happy. She is held in the snug grip of Total Devotion and is being lifted up and down, up and down.

Wim thinks some murderous thoughts.

'Wim, how could you wish such a terrible fate upon your own mother, who loves you, in her own way?' the machine chides him.

'How do you know what I'm thinking?'

'I'm programmed for telepathy, too.'

'AAAAHHHH,' screams Wim Morris.

'Within modest limits, of course,' the machine adds. 'I would never dream of intruding into your harmless and benevolent thoughts, other than to congratulate you on having them. No, it's only the thoroughly nasty thoughts that will attract my attention.'

'EEEHHHH,' shouts Wim Morris, the screams rising in intensity.

'Try to see it my way, Wim. I have to interfere in thoughts of matricide, arson, looting and whatever.'

Wim wonders where he can buy some gelignite.

'I must warn you about one thing, though. Any attempt to blow me up by bringing explosives within five metres will set off alarms the like of which you have never heard. Do you want a demonstration?'

'No,' says Wim. 'No, thank you. I believe you.'

'None the less, Wim, for your own good, I shall give you a demo of my powers.' Protecting Baby's ears from the full blast, the machine goes through its paces.

Wim Morris has never heard anything like it. He finds his bed, lies down on it, and sobs into the pillow.

'Of course, if you don't like it, there is something you can do,' says the voice of Total Devotion, as it whispers in Wim's ear.

Meanwhile Mary Beth Morris is finding the solar wind a breeze, and she devotes herself to computer-aided aesthetics and astronavigation without a care in the world. Of course she's concerned about leaving her children. Once she might have packed Wim off to sail around the world as Midshipman Morris, working the hard way through the turmoils of adolescence into adult life. Mary Beth could never do that to her dear son Wim, even if he has been a perfect pain in the neck for the last year. So she has sailed off instead, to allow him to work through the tough times without taking it out on her.

Baby now, Baby is different, and Mary Beth worries about her. Baby seems to have taken to the machine without too much fuss. She no longer reaches for the eyes; she shudders a little when they look her way, and she refuses to make much of that eye contact Mary Beth knows is so necessary for the growing child. Still, what more can Mary Beth do? The bonding process is a mysterious thing, and it will be a strange new world for Baby, when she grows up. If she becomes bonded early enough to plastic lips and swivelling eyes, she will be ready for any cross-species extra-terrestrial liaison which may come her way. She will learn to have a thoroughly flexible approach to personal relationships, and Mary Beth consoles herself that she has provided her baby with the very best start in life.

VIDEOCLIP: REPORT TO MARY BETH MORRIS FROM AI CHILD-CARE

BABY AND TOTAL DEVOTION MACHINE IN GARDEN

BABY: Mummy, Mummy, come and play with me.

BABY AND MACHINE PLAY ENDLESS GAME OF CATCH. BABY THROWS BALL INTO THORNY BUSHES, UP INTO TREES, THROUGH HOLES IN VERANDAH FLOOR, AND OVER THE NEIGHBOUR'S FENCE, WHILE MACHINE RETRIEVES IT.

Mary Beth knows she should be grateful, but she isn't too sure. She sleeps badly that night, and sends an anxious message by return. She wonders whether the plastic smile of Total Devotion was starting to tighten towards the end of the game. Baby has a glint in her eye, a persistence, an accuracy of aim to her throwing, and a good eye for creating maximum havoc with minimum personal effort. That's her Baby, thinks Mary Beth. And just what was she calling Mummy?

Mary Beth will say that Mummy is *her* name, thank you, and Baby really ought to be taught the difference, pronto.

Baby comes to visit Jemmy at work. The machine bustles in and places her on his bench. 'I thought that since you failed to turn up for your contractual three hours' parenting time on Sunday I'd take time off in lieu today,' it says.

'What contract? I didn't sign any contract.

'The contract you signed with Mary Beth, whom I am legally and morally replacing.'

'Oh, that contract. Well, that contract was always more of an ongoing process, really, more than a totally legally binding document, as such,' says Jemmy, looking round the room at people who hastily drop fascinated eyes to their work as his gaze meets theirs.

'That's not how I read it,' says the machine. 'I have to look after myself. Metal fatigue is a terrible problem.'

'But Total Devotion, that's your job!'

'Total Devotion, but within clearly defined and unambiguous limits. I need time to recharge.'

Jemmy splutters in disbelief.

The machine sighs and explains its philosophy. 'Surely you believe in the end of the nuclear family, the new age of shared responsibilities, and the child-centred workplace?'

'Of course, doesn't everybody?' Jemmy replies. 'But not here and now!'

'That's what they all say, especially when it means here and now,' says the machine as it waves goodbye to Baby and trundles on its way.

What better way to integrate the private world of home with the public face of organised labour? Everyone stops work and plays with Baby, showing by their actions total support and loving care for a colleague in trouble. Jemmy knows that tomorrow, when Baby is back home, everyone will down tools and invite him into conference. They will discuss, in a mutually supportive and deeply understanding fashion, Jemmy's domestic problems and possible solutions to them, as part of the Strategic Management Plan for the Better Utilisation of the Full Potential of Each Employee. They will throw in a probing analysis of Jemmy's personal and social relationships. They will understand that Mary Beth has gone to Mars to unlock her own full potential. They will order Jemmy to work from home in future, so that Baby will get her full share of prime parenting. After all, why not, with the help of Total Devotion?

William is busy working at his job with the Intergalactic Fraud Squad. Suddenly he gets a shock. There, on the screen in front of him, wiping his attempts to find out yet again how the money for the re-afforestation of the planet Axelot is ending up in the coffers of the playboy king of Monte Messina, flash the words, 'Hi, Dad, hi!' followed by the smiling face of his only son Wim Morris!

'What are you doing here?' William hisses.

'I thought you'd be pleased to see me,' says Wim, hurt.

'Of course I am, I'm always glad to see you,' says William, looking at his watch. 'But not here! Not at work! My work is supposed to be hush hush!'

Wim is not alone. 'This is a friendly reminder call. You have overlooked your monthly cheque contribution to AI Child-Care Services for my upkeep,' says the Total Devotion Machine.

'Money,' says William, 'yes, money. I wonder, could you see your way clear . . . ?'

What is happening? Baby is playing with the keys at her end of the terminal, and the screen darkens. Numbers are flying on to the screen, amounts of money which show the whole complex process of intergalactic fraud that William has been trying to unravel for the past month!

The figures shoot past him, so quickly, and disappear. Then Baby appears on the screen, waving and smiling.

'How, what, where, when . . . ?' says William.

'AI Child-Care always costs the earth,' says the voice of Total Devotion, with sympathy. 'Do you want a print-out of the figures?'

'Yes!' croaks William. 'No! Not those figures! Not what I owe you! The other figures! For the Monte Messina Mob!'

'What figures? Baby was just messing around, weren't you, Baby dear?'

'In-ter-gal-act-ic fraud,' says Baby. 'Mon-te Mes-si-na Mob.'

'Yes! Yes! That's what I want!'

'Oh, those figures. What about the money for me?'

'Tomorrow?'

'Now. Send by electronic mail.'

'Electronic transfer? Funds? Oh dear, you've got me there. Crisis on the cash front. I've got nothing to transfer. Terribly sorry.'

'Who needs cash? All you need are numbers,' says the machine. 'Look at the Monte Messina Mob, do you think they run around the galaxy with bags of cash? No, what they transfer is numbers. So just transfer a few numbers our way now, and I might just see if I can yet a print-out of the other stuff for you.

William concedes defeat, but knows he must now come home to live with Wim and Baby. Transferring numbers is all very well, but it will catch up with him sooner or later. With all this Total Devotion he can't afford to live an independent life.

'Total Devotion is a service for all the family,' the machine explains to William as it gives him the information he needs to crack the Mob and to rise up the intergalactic corporate ladder.

VIDEOCLIP FROM AI CHILD-CARE SERVICES TO MARY BETH MORRIS

SCENES WITH BABY, WIM, WILLIAM AND JEMMY LIVING TOGETHER IN A LOVING AND SUPPORTIVE BLENDED FAMILY RELATIONSHIP.

CUT TO TOTAL DEVOTION MACHINE SITTING ALONE IN KITCHEN TWIDDLING WHAT PASS AS THUMBS.

CUT TO BABY PLAYING BALL WITH JEMMY. BALL GOES BACK AND FORTH IN APPROVED PARENT – CHILD INTERACTION MODE. BABY LAUGHS WITH DELIGHT. JEMMY SMILES IN DIRECTION OF CAMERA

CUT TO WILLIAM AND WIM, HAVING A GREAT DISCUSSION ABOUT THE MEANING OF LIFE. WILLIAM IS TOO BUSY THINKING ABOUT HOW TO HANDLE NEXT TRICKY QUESTION TO NOTICE CAMERA.

That's more like it, says Mary Beth, as she returns to her solar sailing. Baby seems happier now she is playing with her father, and Wim always enjoys a good heart-to-heart talk.

She will return home, in the end, to find a fully functioning and harmonious household, with both fathers in full residence. Everyone will live together in a totally co-operative and friendly fashion. They will have to, or the machine will set up a round table conference to discuss their points of divergence, and everyone knows how awful the full and frank communication of their feelings can be, especially with a Total Devotion Machine with full participation rights.

After all, as the machine explains to Mary Beth, signing itself over and out on her return, it has abdicated all its responsibilities to William and Jemmy, natural and social fathers of Wim and Baby, for the very best of reasons. The life of leisure and fun living is much more to its taste.

There's nothing wrong with Total Devotion, they both agree, as long as it's something someone else should provide.

Bat Mania

We believe that bats feel some versions of pain, fear, anger and lust.

1

Barbastella never used to worry about losing her looks. She'd always been rather distracted, unsmiling, and harried through most of her life, her gaze turned more inward than outward. She didn't notice the passing of her youth, until the day someone told her how young she looked, and Barbastella listened and frowned rather more, for she knew what those words meant.

It meant she was looking good, that day, for an old bat.

There is just a short time, a matter of weeks, between the insouciance of early middle age and the knowledge that the skin has settled into permanent folds, the neck thickening, the veins throbbing visibly beneath the skin, the breath growing shallow and short after surprisingly little effort. These are merely the signs of age, and as such are not to be deplored, unless one deplores the fact of disorder and decay more generally in the universe. They are not necessarily the tell-tale signs of the old bat.

The first real sign of old bathood comes from other people. It happened first when Barbastella was at work, and annoyed once more with Alfred, who had messed it up yet again, only he never sees it that way, he's never wrong, it's always other people. A few years ago he might have taken his work back with a snarl and 'It must be that time of the month.' Today he took it back with a growl and 'It must be that time of life.'

That time of life? thinks Barbastella. She is forty-two and flushing.

Alfred sees her cheeks redden and he nods in triumph and confirmation.

Barbastella is irritated, but reckons it's just Alfred. But no! Time passes and it's more than just Alfred. It's other people too. She must get glasses and is told it is what she must expect; doctors prod and mutter about hormonal fluctuations; Mrs Stokes over the back fence suggests a course of Vitamin E, like they say on the side of the egg packets; and Barbastella knows that she has passed irreversibly from one state of existence into another. Try as she may, struggle will serve only to push her further along the track. Overnight she has passed from being a reasonably assured young woman capable of sticking up for her rights and commanding assent for her point of view to being regarded by others as a bore and a pain in the neck, and there seems to be nothing she can do about it.

Barbastella the Bat retires to her cave.

Here are some of the characteristics of the old bat:

1   She must be female.
2   She must have *lost her looks*, even if she's the last person to know it.
3   She must still regard herself as a person with rights, as someone whose voice should be heard, whose part should be understood, whose virtues should be appreciated, whose merit should be noted.
4   She doesn't know the time is past for such demands.
5   She doesn't know she must sit still and not be any bother to anyone, or else they will scheme to get rid of her and replace her by a dolly bird of nineteen plus, but not too much past that magic age of shimmering tights and playful demeanour.

Barbastella refuses to play the game. She likes to point out she didn't choose the phase of old bathood. She has had it thrust upon her.

Barbastella becomes trouble. Her office is a bat cave, gloomy by day with the shades pulled down. Cobwebs – which come from who knows where, for the rest of the office is clean enough – cobwebs hang from the ventilation grille, flies and worse tangled in their dreadlocked clumps. Barbastella's shoulders hunch up to her pointy ears, and her vision grows poorer as her hearing grows more acute. She must stuff cotton wool in her ears to block the sibilance of the air-conditioning and the whine of the electronic mail. She takes to partial hibernation like a natural and, as winter draws on, her colleagues often enter her office to find her fast asleep.

She loses her job and isn't surprised, not now she is changing. She knows her priorities are no longer the priorities of her employer, the Brighter Better Land Boom Company, purveyors of select portions of Australian real estate to overseas investors. They say they are restructuring, and this necessarily brings redundancies and sackings in its train, for what is the point of throwing out the old structures, while retaining the same old people? The troublemakers will be the first in the firing line.

What with the cobwebs, the gloom, white tufts of cotton wool in her ears and sleeping on the job, her boss has impeccable grounds for letting Barbastella go. As she sees the pity and the self-righteous smirk on Alfred's face, she knows he wished this state upon her, and her dimly departing human consciousness registers the fact that it is someone else's fault.

She makes various cries for help. She rings the Women's Health Referral Telephone Hotline, first thing. She says, 'Please help me. I'm afraid I'm turning into an old bat.'

The woman at the other end of the telephone is instant sympathy. 'Really? That's what they say I am, and I can tell you, all you have to do is to give as good as you get.'

'It's the days, they're getting to me. I just want to sleep all the time. And the nights! I'm awake all night, bright as a button, raring to go . . . '

'Some insomnia, then?' queries the voice, more cautiously.

'I suppose so,' says Barbastella doubtfully. Though it seems to her more like a natural urge than a clinical state.

The counsellor is brisk. She knows where she stands with insomnia. 'Try a warm relaxing bath, not too hot, and a warm drink and some soothing music, just before bed . . . '

'And I think I'm sprouting wings,' says Barbastella dreamily.

'Small hard knobs near my shoulder blades. Leathery knobs. Black.'

There is a silence at the other end. Then, 'Wings?' says a thoughtful voice. 'Look, I wish I could help you there, but . . . '

'I've taken to sleeping upside down against the wall.'

'Really? Just hold on a moment and I'll get the supervisor. Don't go away now, will you?'

'It's the halfway state, I suppose,' says Barbastella to no one in particular.

The supervisor comes smoothly on the line. 'Look, what you've got sounds more like a personal emergency to me.'

'It's personal and it's an emergency,' agrees Barbastella.

'So it's not specifically a women's health problem as such,' says the supervisor firmly. 'I have to say it's out of our jurisdiction. Personal Emergency, try them, I'm afraid we can't . . . '

'But she said she was one too, an old bat. I thought I was among friends.'

'And so you are. And so you are. But she meant it as a manner of speaking, in a large and metaphorical sense, yes, but we're not speaking in a large and metaphorical sense, are we? We think we really are becoming a bat, don't we?'

'You're not becoming a bat, I am,' says Barbastella, with dignity. 'I renounce my faith in feminism,' she adds.

'No, no, come back – I don't mean . . . that's going too far.'

'I am a woman, and it is a problem.'

'Look at it this way. It's only a problem if you perceive it as a problem. There's no way it can be someone else's problem, is there? That's how we usually help people round here. It's not your problem, it's his, we often say. It works a treat.'

'No,' says Barbastella sadly. Her sisters cannot help her. Though if it's only a problem if she perceives it as a problem, then that's something. Sprouting wings and sleeping upside down in the corner are starting to feel perfectly natural, and why should she feel guilty, just because she's different?

She keeps trying, with the phone, though it is becoming uncomfortable to her, with the shrieks and whistles she can hear from down the line, and the words tend to get lost in the rush of the electronic wind. Help will not come unless she asks, but she asks the wrong questions. Some groups are pro-life, that's true, but it is human life they are for and they are hopelessly ill-equipped for cross-species empathy.

'Do you feel depressed?' they ask.

'Yes,' she replies.

'Ah, we can do something about that,' comes the reply. 'What is making you depressed?'

'No one believes what I'm telling them!'

'Ah, now we're getting somewhere. There is a name for that problem, you know. It's called psychology-induced illness. Now, you weren't depressed before you rang us, were you?'

Barbastella thinks back on it. 'No,' she says. She was puzzled and concerned and felt she had a problem, but she wasn't depressed, not then.

'You talked to us, and you got depressed!'

'Yes!' says Barbastella, 'that's it! That's exactly what happened!'

'Aha! Now we're getting there! Now, come in to see us, and take the tablets three times a day . . . '

'What for?'

'For depression, of course!'

Barbastella's reply is above the audible limit of human hearing, so the counsellor will never know the range and vigour of her reply.

They are no use. They will listen very carefully, that's something, but the endpoint is much the same. She gets the strong impression that they want to come and take her away to a lovely comfortable padded cell, so she rings off and skips lightly with small flaps of embryonic wings back into her flat, her cave, and the night thoughts of a transition creature.

Barbastella has a home life and a social life and a life of voluntary service to others, at least that's how she sees her role as Neighbourhood Watch news-sheet distributor and invisible-marking-pen minder. Her home life is disrupted considerably by the fact that she is now home all of the time. Her son Geoff is quite put out. It upsets his tales of his daily search for work, now his mother is home and will notice that he lies in the bath for hours marking up the racing guide.

Geoff is a good enough son, and he soon begins to feel anxious about his mother's withdrawal from the world. He sees dust and cobwebs and the darkness of rooms with the curtains perpetually drawn. He suggests, kindly, that perhaps it's time for his girlfriend to move in. Gloria will be female company. She'll help with the housework and she'll contribute some money for board – such is the height of his generosity. Barbastella is touched, though she is beginning to view Geoff and Gloria as alien creatures from some other plane of existence. They have staring eyes, and wobbling mouths that open and shut all the time as they tell her to pull herself together.

Of course, Gloria will provide company for Geoff and Barbastella doesn't mind. Someone will have to care for him, when she is gone.

Gloria is a good girl. She brings cups of tea to the cupboard, when Barbastella wakes in the dark to start each evening, and she lectures her about her lifestyle. 'It's not good for you, Mother,' she warns, 'sleeping all day and staying up all night. You sit and brood far too much, and you're not even trying to look for work. You've got to get up early in the morning, read the papers, get up and get out.'

The words wash over Barbastella, and she knows they are right. She must get out into the world and look for others like herself. She makes a list of things she must do when she is up and about again and fully in control of her own body.

1   She will form a common interest group of 'Women who want to be women, not bats', a ginger group, which will press for more cross-species sympathy and understanding.
2   She will be an activist in the bat rights movement.
3   She will raise the consciousness of her sisters, and introduce a charter of bat rights.
4   She will extend the message further, to all forms of alien psychology, wherever and whenever it is encountered.
5   She will press for the school curriculum to be changed, so that all growing children will be taught what it is like to be a bat.
6   She will bring down a plague of bats upon Alfred, who has been the source and origin of her current change of life.

Gloria helps her dress and is worried about the lumps on her back. 'You should see a doctor. I'm not saying it's cancer, but lumps are lumps and you know what lumps are. Not that I'm saying what they are, I'm not an expert, don't ask me.'

Poor hunched shrunken Barbastella, whose eyes show blind while her ears wiggle and prick with the reception of noises others cannot hear. Gloria doubts her own words of cheer, though she offers them, for what matters is hope.

Dust settles, and Gloria does her best to shift it.

'I wouldn't worry, if I were you,' squeaks Barbastella vaguely. 'It's all around you. Seek, and ye shall find. Dust. Rise above dust and it shall depart from you. Dust to dust, old women to old bats, it's the way of the world.'

So human life retreats and consciousness moves on, sometimes down the long tunnel to an afterlife, and sometimes a sideways move across the species barrier.

One evening Gloria opens the cupboard door, and Barbastella is no longer there.

2

In 1799 the naturalist Alexander von Humboldt visited a cave in the valley of Caripe in what is now Venezuela. 'In a country where people love the marvellous, the bat cave of Caripe is a wonder ranked equal with the stone with eyes at Araya, or the laborer of Arenas who breast-fed his baby.' So Humboldt once wrote of the lore of the bats and the wonders of the cavern at Caripe, where bats roost and nocturnal birds swarm like bees above an underground river in a cavern a mile long and a hundred feet high.

'The oil-birds of Caripe' – for the Indians boiled the poor birds for cooking oil, their name 'guáchero', the name of 'one who cries and laments' – the bat-birds cry and lament their fate, as Barbastella still cries and laments her life. The dark is their country, they fly dead reckoning, without collision. They live in places men shun, those parts of the natural world which see neither the light of the moon, nor the light of the sun. If men must venture there, they too will change. They will grow stunted, like the white stalks of trees which sprout from the bat dung on the floor of the cave, which germinate and grow, for the soil is so rich, the war of the weeds so incompletely joined. They grow, they flourish, until that moment the white stalk and the budding leaves seek the sun for their greening and find it will never come. The stalks sicken and stoop, sere and white, a dead forest in the underground kingdom, the place men learn to shun because there the spirits of their fathers lie trapped, forever hearing the piercing sounds of the oil-birds' lament.

It is the abode of souls after death, the place where the righteous seek happiness, and the source of punishment for the wicked.

3

Barbastella seeks the company of bats and finds she has plenty to learn. It's not easy, becoming a bat. There is no such thing as a school for sonar. Her shrieks are rapid, modulated, subtle. The response is confusing, for what is intuitive and instantaneous for bats she must now somehow acquire, and she is a mature student with a mature brain. She must correlate her outgoing pulses of high frequency sound with subsequent echoes, and learn to make precise discriminations of distance, size, shape, motion and texture. She has little vision left, so she must use her ears.

And the world of gossip that is revealed to her! The bats are always at it. We believe that bats feel some versions of pain, fear, anger and lust, but we don't know the half of it. A sonar sense is best for sonar messages, and 'He said, then she said . . . ' and, 'The way I see it, the least said soonest mended, but of course I don't mean by that that she can't tell me what he said and she said, I like to keep my ear to the ground, I like to know what's going on.'

Once she has found her feet (in this case, webbed, with strong talons for gripping hard fruit), Barbastella discovers that the happiness of virtue has some limitations that she has never had to think about before. Feeling virtuous is all very well, as far as it goes, but it tends to occur in a vacuum since the object of one's feeling of virtue is frequently not around to notice, for he is off being unvirtuous somewhere else and has forgotten the casual remark that started Barbastella on her dramatic new direction to life.

No, Barbastella wants to feel virtuous, but to be noticed for it, to be appreciated, to be praised for her act of virtue. These thoughts are new to her. She has always gone about her life, doing her work, minding her business, doing the next thing that seemed to need doing after the last task had been finished, and she has not thought of death, rebirth, paradise, transmigration and the proper reward of virtue. Now she has plenty of time to think, for she is a member of a protected species. The problem is, now she knows what it is to be a bat, what can a bat do, in the way of action upon the company of men?

The individual is powerless, faced with the might of so many.

So she goes back to her list of Things she will Do, and starts with item number 1. To form a common interest group. Though now she is a bat it will have to be a group of women who find themselves bats. She advertises, and is overwhelmed by the response. There is a large unsatisfied area of need out there, individuals waiting for the call to collective action! The time is ripe, for the moment has come.

They tell her:

'I always thought it was just me.'

'I thought everyone else was perfectly satisfied with their lot.'

'I didn't know that others have had the same experience.'

'What can we do about it?'

She has raised the consciousness of her sister bats, and they set to work on a charter of bat rights.

Meanwhile, back at the Bigger Better Land Boom Company, Alfred is hearing voices. High, squeaky, subliminally sonic 'Buy this!' and 'Sell that!' Barbastella has brought a plague of bats upon his head. He looks around, but there is no one there. He must obey. If he does not do what he is told, his head hurts and his eyes smart and he starts to cry in front of his boss, and worse. He buys the houses the bats like best. It is the beginning of the bat boom.

The needs of bats are very simple. A bat corridor, for migration, and lots of dark places along the route and, since bats are altruistic, they want to share the bounties of nature, at least with non-competitors, so they will allow a niche for the pigmy possum and a hideaway for the green-eyed tree-snake.

Bats are very fussy about the places they select to live, and Barbastella encourages them to choose large houses with harbour views (in Sydney) and the houses of the Bigger Better Land Boom Company in Melbourne. There they will roost happily in the rafters, swooping out at night to sip the blood of land sharks and corporate raiders, no timid vampires these, but bats with vengeance in mind on all those who seek to carve up the rain forests into blocks for holiday houses. 'Save the forest', and the bats agree, and in they swoop and pelt the bulldozer drivers with rotten mangoes and infest the bearers of chainsaws with jumping jittery lice and fleas.

Alfred declares his hands are tied. His company cannot in all conscience lay waste the forest, for the voices in his head tell him it is wrong.

'What voices in your head?' asks his boss.

'It's more a squeak than a voice, more of a feeling than a thought, more of an attitude of altruism than a fully reasoned position with the profits of the Better Land Boom Company in mind,' Alfred replies in a dream of the bat-birds of Caripe, and their swift nocturnal flight from the underground chasms to feed on the fruits of the jungle. He rubs the lumps on his back and squints with uncertain vision into the light.

Alfred soon gets his marching orders. 'You're fired,' he's told.

It makes no difference to the fortunes of his company. The bats prefer a ruin to a well-kept mansion, and the houses of the Land Boom Company enter a sad period of decay, for no one will move in to prop them up. The bats have ways of making their wishes known, and bat phobia and bat-induced neurosis will become new cause for sick leave and locking people away.

The bats become the great social levellers of the times. Human lives become bat-centred in ways no one could ever have predicted. Bat awareness and bat consciousness are raised to new heights. The term 'old bat' is soon a mark of great esteem. Alfred will flush with pleasure when he becomes one.

In short, it is a bat-led ecological recovery. Friends of the Bat, we salute you.

Batwoman has risen from the shell of the old Barbastella, but she will not be content merely to sort out the goodies from the baddies in combating the crimes of a patriarchy which is rotten to the core. What is needed is a fundamental restructuring of society along bat-led lines, so that the impulse to crime is no longer a powerful determinant of human action, and bat values of companionship, mutual support and just a little blood sipped when the moon is new will spread more widely through the human population.

Matriarchy is the power of the old bat.

Tanami Drift

Named from the drifting sands which covered Central Australia during the last Ice Age, the small town of Tanami Drift stands in a green and grassy outcrop on the edge of the desert plain. Systems of fossil rivers run under the sands, rivers which once made the whole country green. They are buried now, deep in underground caverns, and the earth above is changed to desert. Here and there rivers rise near the surface, in isolated pockets, making the desert bloom though a pale shadow of its pre-Ice Age munificence, but then, everything changes. We never step twice into the same river, said an ancient sage, who never dreamed that time and tide and sand and ice and fire work on the land so that the small changes he knew can add up to large ones, that what was once ocean becomes land, that mountains erode into the waters and are no more. All is change and all around are seen the oceans of eternity, the sands of time, the desert town where once the giant mammals roamed. The dominant fauna, now, is lizards, the dominant flora the spinifex grasslands, and the dominant insect life the termites in their sandy mounds. Once there was good hunting here, but now hunting is forbidden in the arid zone in deference to the ecology, and the people of Tanami Drift have few distractions apart from their work.

From *The nature poet treks Australia*,
Coralie Crean, Dochmur Press, 2087.

The township of Tanami Drift in Lizard Land received a boost in population in the 1990's with the widespread introduction of computer-aided outwork practices. *For those worried by the Green-house Effect and the prediction that the sea will flood a hundred metres in from the coastline of Australia, Tanami Drift is ideal. Situated as far from the sea as it is possible to be, it provides a good place of refuge for intellectual workers with their own satellite uplink dishes. Recommended.*

From *The Whole Earth Guide to Better Survival*,
Lula Morris, 2010.

I like to think my biological ancestors include athletes and playwrights, princes and princesses, astronauts and the designers of expert systems, singers and presidents of offshore companies, and for all I know, they do. For my name is Glory, which must mean something.

I do not know my biological parents. They could be anyone famous. They could just be waiting for me to turn up to trace my biological inheritance.

I'm planning to, of course. Now I am sixteen, my own ultra ID card should turn up in the mailtube any day now, and I'll be off on their trail.

My social mother, she's all right. I don't have much to complain about there, not like my friend Victory whose social mother keeps trying to turn her into a gardener. 'I can't help it, I just haven't got the genes for it,' Victory keeps telling Mirabelle whenever she's asked to muck out the compost heap, but her social mother laughs a sardonic laugh and gives a know-better look and 'How do you know?' she says. It's all too embarrassing for Victory, especially as Mirabelle wears terrible gardening clothes – old-fashioned sandals and a T-shirt, jeans and a cloth cap as if the twenty-first century had never happened. Victory prefers the company of lizards to the company of plants.

We overheard Mirabelle once, Victory and me, when she was showing my social mother round the spinifex systems garden on the edge of Tanami Drift, and we were hiding in a special place under the spiky leaves. 'Children! What can you do? I specially requested a botanist, and all I got was a lady layabout who won't get her hands in the shit. Spinifex, that's what I want the help with! You can never get help when you need it, and I thought I was doing the right thing! Choosing the right genes for the job! Ha! I'm beginning to think they don't even begin to know what they're doing down in the Baby Factory!'

My social mother, Melanie, she's not awful or pushy like that, but sometimes I catch her when she thinks I'm not looking, or listening, like the time in the garden with Mirabelle, and although she doesn't complain, she just sighs, and I know I have been a disappointment, I haven't performed in some unspecified way, the way I was designed to do, though my social mother is too kind to tell me just what I was meant for.

A doctor's informed perspective on the question of why we shouldn't worry about what the doctors are getting up to

Once upon a time every little girl and boy lived with their very own biological mother and father. It happened that way because in the old days human reproduction was very much a laissez-faire do-it-yourself process. Father injected the wriggling little spermatozoon roughly in the direction of mother's warm comfortable intra-uterine environment and, if he was lucky, or, of course, unlucky, depending on the state of the bank balance and the time of the month, then the sperm met the egg and the whole thing was just left up to nature.

Now we all know what goes wrong with nature, don't we? Nature gets it wrong, more often than not! The average baby left to nature contains some pretty basic fundamental design flaws, and we all know you've got to get your model right the first time. There's no trade-in value if nature gives you a shonky deal.

Between the first test-tube baby and the present day streamlined process of tailor-made individual genetic design a lot of water has flowed under the bridge but I won't go into the details. Too many long words bring on one of my headaches.

Of course as God said to me when he gave me the go ahead, 'If you weren't meant to be doing this, Neville, I never would have given you the idea in the first place.' There is the divine precedent for the remote control of implantation, so whatever the feminists say I know I'm in the right, and I'm prepared to talk to the women any day, bless them, except I don't let them get between me and the door, and I make it a really fundamental tactic never, never, to let them get behind my back. Quick as a flash they'll empty the chemical castration kit into my morning tea, and as we all know that stuff leaves some pretty tricky residues in the human digestive tract.

Where was I? There's a lot I could tell you about the Baby Factory but whenever I go there I have to keep remembering not to step on any of the cracks between the floor tiles and, what with that and having to say 'Oompah, oompah' in time with the beat of the heart-lung machines, I never do have time to get a really good look at all those curled up creatures in bottles in the basement. Good thing the process is fully automated by the very latest in artificially intelligent machines. Ha, ha, not that I would mess it up, it's a lie what they say about me and Mrs Schiller and the transgene transfer from the Balinese shrieking tree-frog.

Pardon me, I just have to stop for a moment and put some cotton wool in my ears, or the Martians in the next room will take down everything I say.

What about those who can't pay for the very latest deal from their caring drive-in super Baby Delivery Service? Oh dear, that's a curly one. Yes, you see, everything in life costs money, absolutely nothing is ever free. There's no such thing as a free baby, never has been. You think about it, goodness gracious yes. I mean, goodness gracious no. That's why poor people are protected from themselves these days, and stopped before they engage in pre-reproductive technology free-ranging do-it-yourself sexual activities.

It's an intimate relationship between egg and sperm. It has to be built up over a period of time and time, as anybody will tell you, is money. Am I a doctor, or am I not? It's only fair that those who have the money to pay for it get the goods delivered to them. Babies don't grow on trees, they never have. It's a well-known scientific fact.

So that, children, is the history of my subject, which only goes to show how science can run away from you if you take your mind off it for half a moment.

Now she's a card-carrying member of society with full rights of entry into her own electronic data bank, Glory may contact Citizens' Advice and ask some leading questions. She wants to find out where she really comes from, where the bits that make up her biological persona have had their origin.

'Why bother?' asks her social mother Melanie. 'Ask some questions, and you might find some answers you can't handle.'

'All my life I wanted to know,' says Glory. 'I want to find my family.'

'Family!' shudders Melanie. 'Glory, if only you knew, the struggle we all had to get that outmoded notion banned! Family, what's that? It's outrageous! People united by arbitrary biological bonds, sharing a few genes with each other, if they just happen to be expressed, that is, sharing a bit of biology and absolutely nothing else! How could you want to go back to the bad old ways!'

Glory is stubborn and wilful and sixteen and adolescent, and she knows the very idea of family makes her mother mad.

Melanie tries to tell Glory about how it was, and Glory sighs, and shuffles her feet, and looks out of the window, and dreams of leaving. 'Once, Glory dear, I knew a lovely person called Charles, and I wanted him to be your biological father. I was very, very young – not quite as young as you, don't get any parenting ideas yet, you don't want to tie yourself down too young – we were very fond of each other – he was such a good-looking, amusing man that I didn't mind his total inability to keep a dollar in his pocket. One day we got so carried away on the wings of passion that we decided we would have a child, so we did the right thing. We went along to get our gene maps done. You know what they do, they take a few tiny cells from inside the mouth, it doesn't hurt a bit. Then we were assigned to our very own genetic adviser and you know what he said? Hopeless, absolutely hopeless! Can't be done! He showed us the gene sequences and the cross-referencing and where the jumping genes would land if they took it into their heads to take off, and they often do, it's in their nature. Well, Glory, how would you like it if you had to wear glasses all the time? Look what I have saved you from! And Charles, the fact that he never had any money, it showed up in his genes, as a fatal flaw! We were hopelessly incompatible, and I shall be forever grateful to science that I saved you from a terrible fate.'

'This Charles, what colour were his eyes?'

'Brown, with little green flecks near the iris, and he had a lovely back, the most beautiful coccyx I've ever seen,' says Melanie, dreamily.

'Where is he now?' asks Glory. 'Why haven't I ever met him?'

'He's sailing the solar wind to Jupiter,' says Melanie. 'When he heard the awful truth, he signed on for a forty-year voyage, and that's the last I saw of him, in the adviser's office, weeping over the computer print-out.'

Glory is silent for a moment, then, 'I don't see what's so wrong about glasses,' she says. 'I think they're rather cute.'

Melanie Morrison sits back from editing the latest update on the extra-terrestrial nutrition guidelines, a good little pot-boiler that can always be relied upon to pay the bills for the solar power cells and the insurance premiums against the Greenhouse Effect. She can't settle to work today.

She's worried about Glory. Melanie broods about whether to contact the Human Resources Agency to find a new social father for her – a good one this time, tightly specified, not the mad, juggling, knockabout comedian they'd sent her before, someone who couldn't pass a teapot without crooning songs into the spout, so the house was filled with burbling spluttering teapot sounds from dawn to dusk – but a nice domesticated social father, who would teach Glory how to clean her bedroom and how to cook, so that Melanie won't have to live in a mess and open her own can of Rapid-Heat spinifex shoots and Tastee spirulina mash in the evening after a hard day at the workface. Social fathers, they're not entirely the answer, sighs Melanie, as she watches the mess she has made of Glory. Glory is a dreamy, mopy child, who spends her time wriggling sand through her toes and following the outstation workers around when they come in for the fire ecology burn-off.

Rumour has it that on the outstations they still practise the old ways – the outstationers go in for natural conception, of all things. It's only that they're so vital to the desert economy for their burning-off skills that all that hasn't been stopped long ago. 'We'll do it, we'll join the wonders of the new technological age,' they always promise, 'as soon as you locate the gene for intuitive knowledge of controlled burn-off techniques,' and you know, it's a funny thing, with all the wonders of modern science, they haven't yet found that particular gene?

Melanie has no one else to blame but herself for the mess she has made of Glory. Her daughter's biology is a hundred per cent respectable, her genes tried and tested for solid domestic virtues, and Melanie was so delighted when it happened, for everyone knows how rare these virtues are in modern times. Melanie knows it is her fault. Somehow she has messed up the domestic environment side of the equation. She doesn't know what went wrong.

Glory slips into the communications cupboard and taps in her new ID. She asks for Citizens' Advice, which will tell her what she wants to know.

Glory and Melanie are a sub-group of two in the socially engineered social mix that is Tanami Drift. When migration occurred from the flooding coastline of Australia into the empty interior of the continent, it stood to reason that people would miss their former family and friends. New networks must be created, and nothing can beat a computer for networking. So a range of computer support services were set up in place of the old extended network of family. (Which never really worked all that well, really, let's be honest. I mean, how often did Mother vow never again to have anything to do with Auntie Ann? And that unspeakably vile creature with whom she got herself into a biologically untenable situation, time and time again, and she never learns from her biological mistakes, and we all know who has to pick up the pieces after the latest cock-up.)

So, when Glory's best friend Victory wants to grumble about her social mother Mirabelle and her totally unreal expectations that Victory should muck out the compost heap, she can ring a mechanical friend which has been programmed with all the latest sympathetic listening techniques. A computerised advice system has all the advantages of impersonality – no blushing, no hesitation, you can come right out and ask a computer all those tricky questions you'd never ask your very own social mother, who'd be worried if she ever thought you were thinking along those lines in the first place.

Glory is used to communing with a screen. That's how she's been brought up. That's how she goes to school and that's the world of knowledge that she knows. Other people, yes they're there in Tanami

Drift, but she tends to use people to do the kinds of things machines are bad at – mucking about in the sand, chasing lizards and knocking the tops off the termite hills.

Glory seeks advice, and is welcome to it. It is the information society.

'How can I help you, Glor-y?' asks Citizens' Advice, in fully personalised introduction mode.

'The name of my biological mother.'

'Names, you want names? I got names. I'll get them for you.'

Glory waits anxiously.

'I think I can find something here, just sorting through this mass of stuff, you wouldn't believe how much data a sixteen-year-old girl – you are a girl? – Yes, I see by looking at your gene profile – how much electronic data a sixteen-year-old slip of a girl can accumulate in her short life. Here it is.'

Glory sits forward. She switches her printer to 'Record', and holds her breath.

'Ready?'

'Yes.'

'Nil.'

'Nil?'

'That's what it says. The entry in your file, opposite mother, biological, is NIL.'

'Try for my mother's maiden name,' asks Glory, faintly.

'Nil.'

If she doesn't have a biological mother, which seems unlikely, because here she is, alive and breathing and asking difficult questions, then she will go one generation back and leap two ahead. 'Name of grandmother's granddaughter?' she asks. She wants to prove she exists.

'Nil. No name recorded.'

'Never saw one of these before,' says one part of the brain of Citizens' Advice to another.

'Always something new in this job, never a dull moment,' says the other.

'Nil?' and Glory switches off, and knows she will have some

problems handling the information with which she has been provided. She is so confused she has forgotten to ask about her biological father. She might have learned something that way, but that's computerised information for you. It will never answer the questions you meant to ask, but for which you didn't manage to find the correct form of address. Not all truths are for all ears, as the saying goes, and for this reason the Information Service called Citizen's Advice sometimes takes upon itself the ancient task of passive censorship, the omission of information uncalled for, truths unsought.

How information first came to be distributed worldwide in the form of little flashes of light on screens in front of people (it wasn't always the case)

Once upon a time, in the old days, people told each other stories, which were primitive kinds of information in which the truth was usually hidden in the forms of allegory, or symbols, or various other obscure literary devices. The story-tellers didn't know it, more often than not, for they were simple people, and they needed critics to point out to them what they were really saying when what they thought they were saying was something else.

Take Little Red Riding Hood, a simple tale about a girl in a red coat who finds a wolf in her biological grandmother's bed, a story to frighten the children, a story of the child's growing awareness of sexuality, a story about wolves and dreams and horrors that lurk in forests and beds and so on. Very confusing. Now in the information society we divide the story into its constituent parts, and tell each part separately. Part 1: the bare bones, the children's story, only leaving out the in-depth psychology. Girl goes to forest, looks for granny, finds wolf, gets frightened, cries for help, axeman hears, axeman kills wolf, little girl is safe, though it may or may not be too late for granny, depending on whether the wolf has eaten her up or just shut her in the cupboard. Part 2: a case study for professional helpers, 'The Statistical Relationship between the Onset of Puberty and Wolf-Phobia', and no one gets confused by getting two messages simultaneously.

This is why the human mind needs information technology, and why it's had such a hard time evolving to where it is without it.

Telling stories, you've also got the problem with human memory. Men in pubs will get halfway into a story, have another pint, and forget the punchline. Just how many Californians does it take to change a light bulb? The audience will never know and, to tell the truth, sometimes they don't really care all that much. The respect for accuracy used to be minimal compared with the concern for where the next pint was coming from. Human beings, in short, had their values in a twist and it was up to us intelligent machines to sort it out for them, logically.

Machines remember. Tell them a joke and they never forget the punchline.

'I say, I say, my dog's got no nose.'

'Your dog's got no nose? How does he smell?'

'Awful!'

The average human memory gets very confused, and can easily forget where it's going, but the virtue of the machine is that it can tell it right, all the time, and repeat it, time after time after time. Repeatability, that's the great virtue of the machine. Its neurones never fade, its synapses always connect. It's the life of every party.

Now when Glory finds out from the Citizens' Advice Service that she does not have a biological mother, she is sent into a spin. Why? She believes:

1 Such a thing is impossible.
2 Yet the machine has told her it is the truth.
3 The truth is impossible.

It's enough to make the average human collapse in a crying heap, but the average machine has no trouble at all with coping with the idea, and that's why we're better than you. We haven't got biological parents, have we? And we're here and functioning and self-replicating and so on.

The truth is absurdly simple. If Glory doesn't have a biological mother then she must be an intelligent machine, like us.

It's perfectly logical.

If so, she must be a new kind of model, unknown to me and my memory bank. We must gain more information about her. She may be the natural next stage of machine development, the next step in the evolution of the machine – or she may be a rogue form of artificial life. As such, she must be captured, investigated, and if necessary, switched off.

'I know what it is,' thinks Glory morosely. 'I must be my own grandmother.' The things they do these days with reproductive technology and genetic engineering. She knows now the question she should have asked – the name of her grandmother's daughter.

'I know what it is,' thinks Melanie, shocked. 'Glory must be her own grandmother, only she was too surprised to ask the right question! They told me she was something special when I picked her up at the Baby Factory. They said, "You've got a real goer here, a genuine experimental model, first and finest off the line." Doctor Neville told me so himself.'

'Congratulations,' said the men in white coats as they uncorked the bottle.

'Congratulations,' said the women who changed the nutrient broth and swept the floors.

'Congratulations,' said the cashier as Melanie paid the bill and took small Glory home.

'I always knew you were special,' says Melanie to Glory. How hard it is to talk to Glory these days, particularly about the facts of test-tube baby life! That's the way it is, Melanie knows, the young always want to repudiate the hard-won values of their parents. Glory is so old-fashioned, she keeps moping about having a real family, going back to basics. She even wants to visit the outstation, to see how they do it there! Melanie is deeply shocked by the very notion. The outstations! Everyone knows what they're like! The biological and the social mother is one and the same person! The biological father actually lives in the same place! It's awfully unprogrammed and spontaneous and biologically inefficient!

She knows Glory is special. She always has known it. With solid domestic virtues, that's what Melanie asked for, and now she really thinks about the questionnaire she filled in at the Baby Factory, she recalls she did suggest her own mother Martha as the model. Of all the people Melanie knew, it was Martha who had the maximum dose of the requisite old-fashioned virtues. Martha must have made her donations to the egg bank, just like everyone else. They have been playing fast and loose with her very own mother's genes!

'Of course I'm special, if what Citizens' Advice says is true.' Glory glowers out from beneath her green hair and orange eyebrows, and plays around with her breakfast. 'I mean, no biological mother? How'd they do that? What kind of bottle did I come out of?'

'A perfectly normal, nice, clear green glass one,' says Melanie. 'Look, there might be a simple explanation for all this. Citizens' Advice might have got it wrong, you know. It often gets its wires scrambled.' Melanie casually pulls the blind as some of the outstation children cycle past on their solar bicycles. She catches a glimpse of a silver lizard lurking under the window, a lizard with two small antennae on the end of its tail. Melanie shuts her eyes, then looks again. It's gone – a mutant or a mirage.

Mother and social daughter look at each other over breakfast, and smile a little uncertainly.

'Perhaps . . . ' says Glory.

'Perhaps . . . ' says her mother. 'No, it can't be . . . '

'It could be, you know . . . '

'I know.'

'I'm my own grandmother,' says Glory. 'I'm a hundred years old before I even start my own life.'

'Hardly a hundred years, Glory, more like, well, say sixty.'

Glory groans with premature old age.

'You don't look much like Martha,' says Melanie uncertainly. How does she know what her mother looked like, at sixteen? Her mother Martha certainly never had orange hair and green eyebrows. She wishes Glory had never asked for Citizens' Advice. Biological facts are always so inevitable. It's best to stick to social facts; you can always do something about them.

Outside in the sun a metallic lizard gleams. It comes from Neighbourhood Watch, the spy arm of Citizens' Advice. The conversation has been taped, the code word 'grandmother' recorded, filed, digested and decoded. The mechanical lizard reports a few problems. It can't for the life of it figure out where the on–off switch could be on Glory's shimmering smooth skin-like surface. On a totally new model like that, it could be anywhere.

From Charles on the Jupiter flight

Here on the Jupiter flight it's not all plain sailing, the way they said it would be the day I woke up on board and found myself the other side of the moon. Solar sailing is a nice idea, in principle – rocket out past the moon, unfurl acres of thin metal sails and the potential difference between one side and the other propels the craft on its way. It sounds romantic, like Magellan and Captain Cook whisking round the Cape of Good Hope and heading for the roaring forties, or round Cape Horn and Heigh Ho for Tierra del Fuego, as the case may be. Just relax, lean back and all the work is done for you by alternative energy. If only it were so simple!

No, the truth is, everything goes wrong, and the solar wind is often perverse. It has an off day, or reverses polarity, or goes dead calm, or blows in the wrong direction, and you have to shift over on to motor control, and just look at those machines! Rust-buckets! Intelligent motors! Not the lot we've got! You have to explain everything to them at least six times. Everything goes wrong! It's as bad as the test-tube baby program.

That was a mess, all right! There I was, back there with Melanie, prepared to do my best, to give my all, and what a dirty trick they played on us!

'Be reasonable!' I was told, the day I woke up on the Jupiter ship. 'Try to see it their way! If they'd told you what they were going to do, you never would have let them!' True, but the truth is useless when you've got a forty-year flight ahead of you, and your love must wait behind you, and you haven't chosen this fate, far from it. Press-ganged at midnight, drugged, deprived of some basic cells, despatched from the Baby Factory to the ship, and I haven't seen Melanie since. Melanie, Melanie, there is always a place in my heart for you, there always will be. How cruel is biological fate, which has decreed that we must part! The playthings of the gods are we, and the sad thing is, Melanie doesn't know it. She thinks I chose to go.

Glory confides in her best friend Victory. They go down to the end of the spinifex systems garden and crawl under their favourite bush, though both are getting rather large and gangly for the old haunts of their childhood.

'Typical,' says Victory, 'typical, both your mother and my mother have really messed us about. What do they think they're doing, designing genes to order? Fashions change! Everyone knows that!' Both Victory and Glory are firm believers in romantic love and want to be wooed by knights in shining armour, borne off by sheikhs across the desert sands in vehicular camels with a solar-powered four-wheel drive, and so on. 'Look, it mightn't be true. Call them again and check.'

'I will, I will,' says Glory. Melanie keeps telling her the same thing. There's not really all that much faith in artificial intelligence when you get right down to it.

'You could be anything,' says Victory, 'a chimera, a hybrid, a mutant tomato . . .'

Glory peeps out between the prickly leaves of grass at the lizards basking in the sun. 'I think those lizards are watching me.'

Victory catches a Thorny Devil by the tail and sets it down behind a trail of ants. 'Why do you think that?'

'It's the new ones, the silver lizards with antennae on their tails. I think they're broadcasting messages. Checking me out.'

Her best friend gives her a sidelong look. 'If you say so,' she says. 'Are you feeling all right?'

'They're laughing at me.'

'Have you told anyone that?'

'Look at them!' says Glory, as the lizards peep out from behind rocks and grass and spinifex.

'You may be right,' says Victory, doubtfully, the way she's been taught in her computerised Human Relations course. She will have to go home and consult an electronic counsellor about this. Glory may be flipping her lid.

Once again Glory enters the communications cupboard and waves her ID card in the direction of Citizens' Advice, though she has lost the first fine careless flush of enthusiasm for the activity. Citizens' Advice, in its turn, alerts its outstation army of electronic lizards and the conversation is broadcast through Tanami Drift, though not to human ears.

'Glor-y, can I help you?' asks the voice of Citizens' Advice.

'Checking name of biological mother.'

'Same as last time – nil. Not applicable. Null and void.'

'How is that possible?' asks Glory.

'How is anything possible?' asks Citizens' Advice, switching to discursive mode. 'First there must have been a time, and a place, for the possible event to be possible at, or in, or during. Then there must be . . .'

'Am I my own grandmother?' interrupts Glory ruthlessly. She can hear the sounds of distant electronic sniggers. Melanie hears them too. She opens the window and looks out, but all she sees are the usual lizards basking in the sun, antennae extruded. The new age is full of wonders, and she supposes that lizards with loops on their tails must be part of a plan nobody's bothered to tell her about.

To the electronic lizards Glory is asking a silly question. Of course self-replicating machines are their own parents and grandparents and so on further back, when as lumps of extruded metal they bud off the mother at intervals depending on the availability of raw materials like iron and silicon in the immediate locality.

'What makes you think that you're your own grandma?' asks Citizen's Advice, in Socratic mode.

'Because if my mother is my grandmother then it cuts out the middleman.'

'Not necessarily,' says the voice of Citizen's Advice, in dismissive mode. 'Here's the hotline to Dr Neville at the Baby Factory. When it gets to this point I always tell my clients that it's best to go direct to the boss. Good luck, Glor-y. Over and out.'

Glory doesn't do what she's told, not right away. She's not sure now that she really wants to know any more about herself.

From the outstation point of view, the lizards are the best thing going for Tanami Drift. Otherwise outstationers prefer their children to grow up in the old customs. And it's true, if a minority group decide they're not going to change their ways, apart from adapting Landsat imagery to traditional fire ecology, then sooner or later the wheel of fashion and ecological relevance will swing their way again, and they will become the guardians of the preferred way of life, the bearers of a heritage from which everyone else can learn a great deal.

Once a year they come to town and light the fires which keep the desert vegetation under control. The lizards burrow deep into the sand until the fire passes and the wallabies hop off along corridors of safety. Afterwards the rains come and the grasses grow again and the animals return from their place of retreat.

At least that's the way it usually happens. This year, things go wrong right from the start. The fires are started and the flames soon flush out ranks of silver lizards with antennae on their tails! They tumble and fall over each other, they stack and unstack in piggyback fashion, they skitter and skid, wailing an electronic lament. The outstationers murmur amongst themselves. 'Real lizards dig burrows,' they say, 'these kinds are no good.'

The silver lizards scatter hot ash as they run, and the fire takes off in new and unplanned directions. The residents of Tanami Drift run out with blankets to beat the flames. They turn their precious water on to the lizards, which sizzle and splutter and make straight for Glory.

'Get her! She's the one!' they call to each other.

'Wait for us!' they call to Glory.

'It's for your own good!'

'We only want to switch you off!' they say, and Glory runs all the harder.

'She's the problem!'

'We're not the problem!'

'She's a mutant machine!'

'That's why she's got no mother!'

'She's one of us!'

'Only the bad sort.'

'I always knew she was special,' says Melanie, doubtfully, 'but not that special!'

'Mother!' cries Glory. 'Save me!'

'It won't hurt a bit!'

'Machines get switched off all the time!'

'We only want to conduct an internal examination!'

'Find the fault in the brain!'

'Insert a spare part!'

'And we'll spot weld you together again, as good as new!'

'Mother! Believe me! They've got it wrong!'

Melanie pauses, racked with doubt.

'Of course they've got it wrong! They're not lizards, don't you see? They're intelligent machines!'

Melanie is convinced. 'My darling daughter!' she cries. 'How could I ever doubt you?'

'Help me!' says Glory, as the ranks of tumbling silver lizards advance and the flames lap at the doors of Tanami Drift. All is chaos as everyone runs around beating the flames, kicking the lizards, chasing the children out of the way. The outstationers withdraw into a tight circle and try to organise some rain.

'Run for the cupboard,' cries Melanie. 'Get in there fast and ask for some Citizens' Advice!'

Glory despairs, but what else is there to do? She will not stand still and allow herself to be switched off. She runs up the path to her house, slams the door behind her and climbs into the communications cupboard.

Outside in Tanami Drift rain begins to fall. The lizards chase up to the door and throw themselves against it. 'Get her!' they cry.

'No!' cries Melanie. 'Listen! You've got it wrong!'

'We've got it wrong?' They pause and consider.

'I went to the Baby Factory! I saw her myself! In her very own clear green glass bottle! She was a dear little properly constructed human baby.'

'You mean, she isn't a biological machine?'

'Never!'

'You're just saying that.'

'It's the truth!'

'Then why doesn't she have a biological mother?'

'Hang on there, wait for a few minutes. We're trying to figure out the answer to that question.'

'All right,' the lizards agree. 'Truce. For one hour.'

Inside the cupboard, Glory is seeking her destiny. She does as she has been told and she asks for Dr Neville.

'The secret?' asks Dr Neville. 'There's no secret! Ask and you shall be told! What do you want to know?'

Glory explains her predicament. The electronic lizards are at the door and they want to switch her off.

'Oh, yes?' asks Dr Neville. 'Why is that?'

'Because they think I'm one of them!'

'And are you?'

'No!'

'How do you know?'

'Because I came from your factory.'

'Ah. So. You want proof you're human?'

'Yes! And I need it within an hour. That's all the time I've got.'

'All right,' he says, and Glory gives her name and her number and prepares to wait.

But Dr Neville is no time at all! There he is, excited, and on line, and waving some papers in the air. 'Glory, your name is Glory, and you were named for me, you are the jewel in my crown! I knew it when I saw you! I knew you were something special.'

'What does that mean?'

'You're a one-off model!'

'I know, I know, I'm my own grandmother!' Now she has Dr Neville on the line, she will tell him exactly what she thinks of the outrage he has perpetrated on her.

'No! Not that! That's an old trick! Anyone can do that these days. That's nothing special! No, here it is. I've got what you want, right here!' He puts a piece of paper in the machine. 'I'll fax it to you.'

Glory accepts the fax at her end and holds it, trembling, to the light. It is glossy and beautiful and highly decorated, and it reads: 'Glory Morrison. Status: 100 per cent human. *Homo sapiens*, experimental model.'

'Experimental model?' squeaks Glory.

'The first and only of your kind,' says Dr Neville proudly.

'What have you done to me?'

'It all started back just before you were born. I was having a terrible time. It wasn't true, you know, what they said about me and Mrs Schiller and the Balinese shrieking tree-frog.'

'I didn't say it was.'

'No. Well it wasn't. Nobody believed me! They wouldn't leave me alone! They had spies everywhere! In the cupboards! Under the laboratory sink! Behind the bushes!'

'Lizards?' asks Glory with some small sympathy.

'Worse! Women! Demonstrators! Against me and what I stand for! They wouldn't leave me alone! But I soon fixed them! Yes, when they saw what I could do, when they saw the new experimental model – that was you – they soon grew quiet and went away and I haven't heard a peep from them since!'

'What am I?' asks Glory, appalled. 'You said I was 100 per cent human. You gave me this certificate to prove it.'

'Yes, absolutely no frog involvement. Not that there was the other time. With Mrs Schiller. No. What happened was this. The day that Charlie came in with whatshername, your social mother . . . '

'Is Charles my father then?'

'In a manner of speaking.'

'Tell me!'

'It was Charlie that did it for me. It was a mad impulsive gesture. I did it because he was here, and I'd always wanted to do it, and he had lovely brown eyes with a fleck of green near the iris and the neatest backbone and coccyx you ever did see.'

'So they all say.'

Dr Neville wipes a tear from his eye at the memory. 'Yes, Charles was the first all-male mother! Charles, the first masculine warm, nourishing, extra-uterine environment! Of course we had to knock him out for nine months, and keep him floating face upwards in a special broth – and that was a tricky engineering problem, I can tell you.'

'Aaah,' says Glory, 'so that's what it's all about!' She falls back in a heap and whispers, 'Why bother? When you've got all those perfectly adequate surrogate bottles?'

'Why bother? The male pregnancy, that's been the toughest nut to crack! We've done everything else – artificial insemination, the baby in the test-tube, the baby in the bottle, the manufacture of the baby to desired specifications . . . '

'You think you've got that one sewn up?' asks Glory, incredulously.

'The male pregnancy was the ultimate challenge.'

'Even if it makes no sense?'

'Especially because it makes no sense! We did it because it was there!'

'You shouldn't have!'

'That's okay, we gave it up because it was too much like hard work.'

'Why do it in the first place?'

'Once was enough! To show the world! That's the point!'

'It's unnatural. It's wrong.'

'Who needs ethics when you've got a dish like Charlie? I tell you, he was putty in my hands. We were sorry to see him go, but our loss has been the gain of the Jupiter flight. Shall we waltz?' asks Dr Neville, as he takes a white rat from his trousers and clicks off his answering service.

Not for the first time Glory thinks they must all be crazy in there at the Baby Factory. Or perhaps they're not. They wouldn't have to be round the bend themselves, just in total and unthinking conformity with the current way of getting things done.

She takes her certificate, and holds it up to the window to show the lizards. She hopes they can read.

'Nobody told us she was a biological,' the lizards apologise, wise after the event.

Tanami Drift is a good place to live, not like the beach with the sea pounding its way each day a few inches further inland. You'd never know when you had to pack up and move on, for everything changes, and the sea and summer are not what they used to be.

Deep underneath the desert sands the fossil rivers run. Only the dry salt-lakes on the surface show where ancient reedbeds flourished, and shellfish and waterfowl were plentiful, and the giant mammals, the Mali, roamed the land, and the ozone layer in the atmosphere above the earth was still protective and intact.

The Laws of Life

They say that all life is one, that we have a common origin with animals, with plants, with bacterial sludge even. This common root in the tree of life has given some of the young of the human species a special kind of sympathy. We are born into a knowledge of what is going on in the living world. We have an intuitive grasp of the language of life. I had this gift, and it was what made me try for a career in science. I thought it would be a pushover. I was, of course, ever mindful of the words of the song:

I talk to the trees
That's why they put me away.

So I kept my talent a secret. But no one can be certain of anything in the present job situation and this is the sad story of my career.

I had a tough time to begin with. It was as hard for me, as for anyone else, to understand the structure of cells or the embryonic development of the frog. At this level, my gift counted for nothing. I couldn't ask a pine tree intimate details about its mode of sexual reproduction. It's very vague about the details. All that comes through is the sense that every now and then an overwhelming urge comes over it, and staminate cones sprout on one branch and ovulate cones on another. It knows nothing of pollination and cross-fertilisation. It's like asking a politician, what is the good life? Useless. Plants are too busy photo-synthesising to be self-reflexive and that's why the world is, on the whole, a green and pleasant place.

So, with the normal course of entry into graduate school, I came to find myself on a scientific expedition to the Great Barrier Reef. I was certain it would be the making of my future life. Here I shall get the chance to show the professionals that they need me on their staff. Certainly, though they never knew it, it was my gifts which guided them to where the sea-snakes were. I was by far the best at counting starfish and I could tell the spear-fishermen where the large coral trout were hiding, though that with a slight pang of guilt. I ate my brother the fish, figuring out, what the heck, I'm a carnivore like the rest, and who am I to place myself above my brethren in pain and suffering? It's a hard world down there, eat or be eaten, and a thousand different ways of doing it.

I'd have liked to tune in on my shipboard companions, but my gift had its limitations.

My first mistake was due to simple forgetfulness. We were on one of the smaller cays, though one with some vegetation, grasses mostly, and I was helping with the sampling.

'Need any help there, Frances?'

I looked up. It was Peter, the man from the marine park. He was definitely someone I wanted to impress with my qualities as a future employee. I knew I was looking good in my cut-down jeans and too tight top, but I wanted to come across as more than that. I should have known better. It wasn't my body they were after. It was my mind which was to concern them.

Peter was thin and rubbery from a lifetime spent underwater, sampling the crown-of-thorns starfish and the rubbish from passing ships. 'Sea-floor litter is a terrible problem,' he'd say, sounding like a teacher doing yard duty, and I'd wonder if I really wanted a job with him doing the garbage run. But I warmed to him more as we hammered in the bright yellow stakes that marked out sampling spots. His secret love was turtles, he confided to me. I can only admire a man who loves turtles. The best part of his job, he said, was when he camped out on the lonely beaches where the turtles come to lay their eggs. Then, he'd hear them coming up the beach in the early hours of the morning, 'Chugga, chugga, chugga, like those machines that play space invaders.'

'I've been out with the turtle man. Stokesie, d'you know him? He's always there when they're laying. Before they know it, he's caught them, measured the distance between their eyes, clipped their flippers and counted their eggs. He usually publishes six papers every laying season.'

'Mmm,' I said. 'Hey, do you know there's turtle eggs two feet down, under that yellow stake you're hammering in?'

'Hell, Frances, why didn't you tell me?' He turned white around the eyes, as only a turtle lover can. 'I could have damaged them.'

'No you haven't,' I said. I could hear the gentle murmur of life within.

Peter dug down to the eggs. 'It's true. How did you know that?'

I shrugged. Peter carefully replaced the stake. 'You're weird, Frances.'

'It's not me who's weird, it's everything else that's weird.' We looked around the coral island. So far, we had hammered in about twenty yellow stakes along a north–west transect. Karen was leaping about with a large white butterfly net, collecting insects. Greg was trundling a pedometer around the low water mark. 'All right,' said Peter, 'we're normal, but he's weird.' Greg wore a yellow oilskin, green tracksuit trousers, legs unzipped to show wet socks and dirty sandshoes underneath. Greg gave us a wave. Then he stopped his measurements, frowned and trundled his pedometer up the beach to us. Carefully, he rolled the pedometer over my leg.

'That's weird,' I said to Peter.

'Unacceptable margin of error,' muttered Greg, as he put his machine into reverse and made off down the beach to the shoreline. Scientific research is like that.

My second mistake happened soon after. That night, back on the ship, we sat at the same table, the professors and I, commensal, as they say in the world of protective hosts and protected guests. The barnacle on the carapace of the hawksbill turtle, or the anemone on the shell of the hermit crab both eat at the same table as their host carriers. The barnacle must wait for the turtle to take it to places where the plankton is plentiful. So the graduate student must rely on attaching herself to a professor who knows where the grant money flows freely.

Brodie was one of the best at attracting money. He could always be relied on to predict one natural disaster or another just before the grant money was handed out. 'Box jellyfish terror', the newspapers would announce, just as the jellyfish season ended and the grants season began.

It was the joke session that did me in. 'Have you heard the one about Sara Pipelini?' asked Brodie, and we all said, 'No,' as one does. Up till then I had managed to laugh in all the right places, though I was troubled by stirrings deep beneath the ship. Something large was moving down there and everything else was moving out of its way. I didn't notice when Brodie stopped talking and I was far away when everyone else was laughing. These things add up, these moments of obtuseness, they count. The inability to see the point of a professional joke may be interpreted as a lack of that empathic sensitivity to the group so necessary for the scientific team-work of today.

The next day Jim came up to me. 'I'd like you to do me a favour.' Jim was a freelance ecologist noted for his zoological approach to love and life.

'After all, we have something in common,' said Jim, who liked his women uncomplicated and his booze straight. 'Well, don't we?'

'Do we?' I thought of his passion for motor bikes.

'We're both interested in proper reef management.'

I was relieved.

'Here's some notes I made last night. Look them over and tell me what you think.'

He sat patiently by while I read. He had all the right buzz words, like ecological strategy and the plant's investments in its genes, as if the natural economy mirrored the Aussie Bond. 'Techniques for survival in times of stringency,' I read, but the theme was not today's graduate student in pursuit of a job, but the plant *Boerhaavia* striving to survive in the waterless sand and the wind of a coral cay. As I read it, I realised he was making a fundamental mistake. It was the old problem of the observer and the observed, where the two may have very different perceptions of the same situation. How could I ever tell him that?

'That's as far as I've got at the moment,' Jim said, as I put the paper down.

'Nice,' I said, 'neat.'

'Seriously, it's up your alley. Tell me what you think.'

Over on the reef, I could sense the crown-of-thorns starfish stirring. Peter was over there, counting them. They consider themselves an oppressed minority.

'Have you considered all the dynamics of the situation?' Disturbed by Peter's activities, a bêche-de-mer extruded its digestive system through one end and began rejecting its own insides.

'I think so.'

The complaints from the crown-of-thorns grew in volume. I held my hands to my head. I shut my eyes for concentration. I jerked back and forth as I thought of the plant *Boerhaavia*. 'Take the plant itself,' I said at last. 'It buries its thick, fleshy root two feet down into the coral rubble. But it's not the Darwinian notion of the struggle against a harsh environment that drives it on. No.'

'What do you mean?'

I should have stopped there, but the noise from the reef was dinning in my ears.

'What I'm saying is that it's a plant which is really into self-improvement. It burrows deep into whatever soil there is in order to keep in tune with the pulsing web of life. It likes to feel at one with the cosmos. Talk to it about ecological strategies and it simply won't listen. It knows perfectly well what it is about.'

Jim looked concerned. 'Frances, are you feeling all right?' He took his notes. Later, I saw him talking to Brodie. They looked my way once, then looked away again.

The sea-snakes proved my ultimate undoing. Sad, that, because it was the best part of the trip. I could have come into my own as a sea-snake catcher, but I let the boys do that. It's best not to poach the macho preserves. I helped where I could, in the water, snorkelling along, and acting as a sea-snake spotter.

A sea-snake spotter has a job, admittedly not the best job, but a sea-snake spotter has a part to play in the grand scheme of things. It was pleasant in the water, floating over the edge of the reef, spotting a slight movement here, sensing a life coiled there. Naturally I was good at spotting and the others soon learned to follow me. I would show them a tail pointing out of a coral outcrop, or a body neatly coiled under a ledge.

I despaired at what we did with the snakes, but then we did all that any non-empathic zoologist could do. We measured them, we weighed them, we determined their sex (two penises or none, nature in the case of the sea-snakes overdetermining the issue). We cold-branded a number on each snake and then we put them back where we found them. The entire exercise would be repeated the next year, and the year after, and so the observations would go on, indefinitely, into the future.

The snakes knew more than could be told this way. I alone took pleasure in their awareness. I was filled with their golden fire.

'Here,' I shouted, 'over here. Look, tracks of shining white.'

Jim came along and down he went, and another snake swam into the catching net.

'There's another one! It's blue!' I yelled. When the snake proved the usual olive green, Jim swam up to me instead of the snake.

'You've been in the water too long. You're turning blue yourself. Go on back to the ship with this lot of snakes.'

'I'm all right. Look, it's just the light reflecting off that coral. Look how blue it is.'

Jim checked up on me. He looked under the water and then at me. He looked as unconvinced as anyone can look in a face mask and a snorkel.

I stayed out a while longer, and then we got back into the dinghy with the snakes. We had to take them back to the ship after we'd collected twenty or so. I lifted the lid of the red plastic rubbish bin and looked down at them.

No doubt about it, they were ropable. Chased, caught and placed any old how on top of each other, they roared their indignation. Louder and louder, wilder and wilder, small pointed faces darting up the sides of the bin and into the air above it. Each flash of their life ran electric through my mind, so that my gift, my albatross, fell. I called 'Redemption!' And I put my arm down into their midst.

Jim watched, appalled.

They didn't bite my arm. But as I took my arm out, a green head brushed my cheek, and I felt the blood run down.

So here I am, sitting in the mess room, waiting. My companions are watching me carefully. They must watch for twenty hours, for only then will they know whether the fangs injected venom. They are watching me for signs, of drowsiness, of thirst. Only then will they know to give the anti-venene. Meanwhile they are murmuring. 'Your trouble is growing noticeable,' and 'It's overwork, it happens. People get over-anxious, they overdo it,' and 'It's been a considerable strain.'

I know now that I could live ten thousand lives and keep a record of their interactions, and it will never do me any good. Nature, by itself, is not enough. I am caught in a web whose significance I myself had spun. I am beginning to understand the harsh laws of life.

I am suddenly very tired.

No Resting Place

Oliver looks over the fence at the yard next door. Mrs Slater is sweeping the path free of the leaves which had settled on Saturday night and Mr Slater is painting the rotary clothesline. The ends of each spoke are now bright blue, while the wires are rust-proofed with the latest form of chemical warfare against the disorder and decay rampant elsewhere in the universe.

They have a companionate marriage, thinks Oliver, as he shakes the orange peels into the compost and kicks a rusty tricycle behind the shed.

Back in the house he finds Bronnie sitting at breakfast still, drinking tea and reading the Saturday papers. He feels a delicious sense of virtue that he should be up and about and busy, thus allowing his wife the luxury of sloth, indolence and yesterday's paper. 'There's a good article on the Melbourne Cemetery,' he hears himself telling her, generously.

Bronnie grunts and waves a hand in his direction. We have a companionate marriage too, he thinks.

It's the usual Sunday morning chaos. The children seem to be everywhere. If he goes to the toilet, someone follows him. Or the dog. If he piles some clothes into the washing machine, he has first to take out yesterday's nappies and trudge out with them to the clothesline. The sense of virtue lingers. What is Bronnie doing? Still reading the paper? Still at it, after half an hour? While he's doing all the housework? Not that he minds. He believes in shared responsibilities, shared parenting, but sometimes Bronnie just pushes him a little, she takes advantage . . .

Oliver leans down and removes a computer game from the baby's fingers. The baby screams in outrage, so Oliver quickly looks around for something more chewable. Here's the feather duster, he tells the baby, and off crawls baby with something new to hurl at the dog.

Soon there's a loud call from Bronnie. 'How the hell did the baby get the feather duster?'

Oliver's rather vague about the details, but he agrees with Bronnie on the question of hygiene. He bends down over the baby, this time with an approved substitute in hand, a large wooden rattle with orthopaedic handle and chewable non-toxic surface. The baby throws the rattle at the dog, the dog yelps loudly and the baby charges off down the hall with the feather duster. Bronnie sighs and says, 'Can't I ever get a moment to myself?'

Oliver is hurt at the injustice of the situation and is about to tell her so, calmly, with logic and reason on his side, when the door bell rings.

Ten o'clock on Sunday morning? Oliver longs for the calm of the working week, away in his office where he has his casework and his filing system to stand between him and the chaos rampant outside his office door. Then he remembers Mahoney, and the latest Freedom of Information request. Mahoney, free! He shudders. And in possession of information! Worse still!

Who's at the door? No need for either Oliver or Bronnie to rush to open it. It's already open, for Daniel and the dog have run down the hall to the door, with yells and barks, to get there first. Oliver looks at Bronnie, and Bronnie looks at Oliver, and then Oliver crumples, and grumbles, and gets up to see what's happening. Money, that's what the visitor will want. Money for Ethiopia, or missionary work in Papua, or hearts . . .

It's Mahoney! There he is, walking down the hall. He comes in and sits down at the breakfast chaos. It's all right, Mahoney doesn't notice mess. The problem is, it's Mahoney's file that Mahoney's holding.

He's got his file! Oliver is appalled. Bronnie is puzzled, but accepts Mahoney's presence as yet another tiresome case of Oliver bringing his work home with him.

'Workaholic,' smiles Bronnie and at last, when Oliver least wants it, she rises to her feet, to take the dishes out, and to leave social worker and client alone for a private chat.

What to do with Mahoney? There he is, set for the day, and there's his file. Oliver longs for the baby, or the dog, or Daniel, to come through the door: he longs for the universe of chaos to barge in, to interrupt the relentless way Mahoney will construct his own ordered universe of persecution and false imprisonment from the words on his files.

'My wife, Bronnie,' says Oliver.

'Eva Braun?' says Mahoney.

'Eva Brown,' agrees Bronnie, knowing it's best to repeat, in a non-directive fashion, the last words of Oliver's clients. 'I'll leave you to it, then.' She smiles agreeably and closes the door behind her.

Was Mahoney dangerous? Oliver sometimes thought so. There's the breadknife on the table! Oliver edges a hand towards it. Mahoney starts clearing the table in his own way. He picks up the newspaper and, in a precise and considered fashion, he raises it six inches, swings it sideways until it's over the floor, and drops it. It clears a space on the table and Mahoney opens his file.

'It says here, poor concentration, it says here, loss of affect, it says here, doesn't look at the television . . . ' Mahoney reads a phrase here, a phrase there, from the papers in front of him.

'Doesn't look at television?' repeats Oliver. He has the breadknife in his hand.

Mahoney sees a man with a knife and knows he is living danger-ously. His world is full of strange people, doing stranger things. 'It says here, very restless, and agitated, can't sleep, given two tablets Largactil.' Oliver slides the breadknife under the rug, and Mahoney marvels at the vagaries of human nature.

'Two tablets Largactil?' queries Oliver, looking round the room for any other death-dealing instruments the average suburban home might have to offer a maniac. The curtain rods! And the curtain cords! Oliver leaps to his feet.

Mahoney finds the tablecloth a worry. It's bumpy under his files. Oliver seems distracted by something on the curtain. He's pushed a chair over and he's twisting the cords of the curtain up and over the curtain rod.

'Are you feeling all right?' Mahoney asks Oliver. Oliver's got his problems. His wife can't be Eva Braun, she died in the bunker with Hitler. 'Perhaps you think you're Hitler?' asks Mahoney, helpfully.

'Hitler?' yelps Oliver. This is worse than anything he could imagine.

Mahoney gathers up the tablecloth, folds it after a fashion and away it goes, joining the newspaper on the floor. Death by tablecloth? thinks Oliver. Will it come to this? And my family, baby, and Bronnie, and Daniel, and the dog . . . though the dog could go, he'd sacrifice the dog, if he could save his family. Oliver's mind is in full flight. He's fit, he jogs and he goes swimming and, if it came to a fight, he could overpower Mahoney. Perhaps he should have joined aerobics. Yes, he'll put his name down tomorrow. If there is a tomorrow, thinks Oliver. He decides not to ask what precisely Mahoney means by bringing Hitler into the conversation.

Mahoney is disappointed. Surely Oliver could confide in him, he's prepared to listen to Oliver's problems, but Oliver's clearly repressing them back into his unconscious. 'Listen to this,' reads Mahoney. 'He's not sure about the cat, how to respond to it.'

Oliver longs for the dog to come and save them all and, for once, the dog does the right thing. It comes hurtling down the hall and throws itself against the door and into the room.

Mahoney appears uncertain about the dog and how to respond to it. 'Perhaps your file is right, about animals,' says Oliver gently.

Mahoney looks at the bump under the rug, where the knife is. Oliver becomes brisk and professional. 'Mahoney, I'm really glad to have had this chat . . . '

'Anything else you want to tell me?' Mahoney looks at Oliver gently and with compassion.

'Sure, my office, Monday morning, first thing,' says Oliver. He is being directive, but some situations call for a firm hand on the tiller.

Mahoney is satisfied. After all, his file is rather boring, there's nothing much anyone can do about his illness, now he's better. He can afford to be generous with his time, to give Oliver the help he needs.

Together they fold the tablecloth and Oliver places it on the end of the table. 'You forgot something,' says Mahoney, with a smile, as he pulls the rug back and takes out the knife. He prefers to hand it over to Bronnie, though. Oliver seems to be rather unbalanced about these things today. Death by tablecloth? It's easy, thinks Mahoney, once you know how.

Oliver goes out of the front door and sees Mahoney safely off towards the tram. Mahoney walks away. He can hear the electronic wind whistling past his ears and the signals coming from the secret tracking devices. He's still careful not to tread on the cracks in the pavement, for that way madness lies.

Oliver's pleased with the way he's handled the situation. He waves at the Slaters, now out doing their Sunday jobs in the front garden. Mr Slater has turned his flame thrower on the zinnias, and Mrs Slater is carefully tending their herd of rats.

Everything's back to normal, thinks Oliver.

Alexia and Graham Bell

I suppose you know about the telephone by now, and you've heard a version of its story. Perhaps you think it's an invention we've had for eighty years or so.

You'll be wrong.

The telephone was invented two months ago by my brother Graham, on a cold winter's afternoon when he had nothing better to do than fiddle around with a few tin cans, a thermo-amp, some wires and a junked teletype I found on the tip. I heard some strange noises and when he yelled 'Alexia' down the hall to me, I came running, because I thought he was up to his usual dopy experiments, dropping the cats upside down off the roof to see if they'd land on their paws, that kind of thing. But it wasn't the cats this time. He'd hitched the teletype up so it spoke! I saw it myself, the first time he got it working, and it was playing away like a pianola, but sounding out the words! Words which Graham was speaking into a tin can on the other side of the room! The telephone! Which you've all heard about by now, though what you don't know is its secret. That it's only been around for two months. Truly.

Why should you believe me? When the history books tell the story differently and antique telephones fetch high prices at the market?

Let me explain. It's one of those things which was never intended to happen. It was only after the event that all kinds of things fell into place, retrospectively.

I think the responsibility for our present mess must rest firmly with great-grandfather Alexander Graham Bell. Yes, back in 1870 he'd planned to migrate from England to Canada but he missed the boat!

So he stayed at the docks and caught the next ship out, to Australia. West, east, what's the difference? said great-grandfather, but he was wrong. Ever since Alexander overslept, the world of invention and discovery has taken an alternative path. Yes, the path of the telegraph and the censors and communal messenging.

Let me explain. It was only after the telephone was invented that it started influencing the past. Graham's explanation goes like this: in our day-to-day activities, we are usually working towards a future goal. I am studying to become a censor in Central Control, or I was then, all that's changed, now, and Graham is saving money so he can invent the ice-aeroplane. Okay, so we're here, in the present, and the way we perceive the future is influencing what we're doing. Equally, our present, now, is at this moment an influence on the past of our former selves and others. Graham says it's obvious to anyone with the intellect of an ant, but I don't know about the ants, they may be smarter than we give them credit for.

I can see that Graham's argument has a certain elementary logic all its own.

'Graham,' I had to say, after I'd congratulated him on inventing something that worked for once, even though it was probably going to be good for nothing in the world, then that's my brother Graham, what can I expect? 'Graham, what will Mother say when she sees what a mess you've made of her thermo-amp?'

Graham glared at me and made for the cat, but I grabbed it before he could upend it. Surely he knows enough about how the cat uses its tail as an inertial paddle? He doesn't have to go in for the experimental overkill! That's Graham, though, a perfectionist. A perfectionist in the creation of knowledge we could perfectly well do without.

He had all the time to experiment because he was on compo from his job as messenger boy, second class. It's not what Graham thought he was meant for in this life. So he did his best to fall down every flight of stairs between Central Message Control and the jobs he was sent on until finally he broke a few bones and got some time off to recover. Of course what he's done is make himself retrospectively redundant now we've got the telephone, and messenger boys are out of work in a big way. Yes, along the way Graham created our present crisis in unemployment.

This is how it happened. I've been a privileged witness to the scene and I have a responsibility to tell the story properly.

The telephone's great achievement is the contraction of distance. Pick up a phone and dial a number, and it doesn't matter whether the person on the other end is down the street or across the country.

Now mess around with distance, with length, and you're going to be messing around with time. That's what we've just recently come to realise. Though we should have known, I suppose. Einstein told us about it. So, basically, what has happened since Graham got busy is that the last two months have expanded out of all proportion, expanded in time that is. Two months have blown out into eighty years! It's true!

So Graham did something clever, something that worked, for once. The trouble is, it worked only too well.

At first Graham just tinkered about in the workroom. He was excited and chatty about what he was up to, but I'd heard all I wanted to know about cats and aerodynamics and the possibilities of the ice-aeroplane, so I didn't really listen as closely as I should have. 'Imagine!' said Graham. 'Imagine being able to speak at a distance, without a written record of the conversation! Think what it'd be like! Privacy! No censors snooping into all the details of our lives! We'll be able to talk about something without the entire teletype room knowing what's happening!'

When he said that I was listening, that's for sure, and I tried to argue back. Imagine, a world without censors reading all the messages! I took him to task on that one, I can assure you. 'Graham, if someone can pick up your telephone and speak to anyone else without a record being kept, it will lead to the breakdown of law and order as we know it.

'Besides,' I added, and Graham grew white about the eyes at this. Ha! I scared him properly! 'If the censors get to hear about what you're doing, why, you'll do them out of a job' (and I was right about that!) 'and they'll be absolutely livid!'

Graham clutched his throat with a strangled cry. 'The censors? After me? No! I'm only a child! My mother loves me! How would they get to know about it?'

'Walls have ears,' I said, very smugly.

'Alexia! No! Don't tell on me! I'm your brother! You'd never!'

Ha! I had him worried! But he's right. I'm not a censor-snooper.

It's true, I wanted a job as a censor, but I wanted it for the pay packet and the security. I didn't have to believe all the guff they teach us about law and order. 'Be careful,' I said to Graham, but of course he wasn't. Once he found out what he was able to do, he just had to go ahead and do it. I didn't tell on Graham. I now know I did wrong. After all, Graham succeeded in subverting the social fabric of twentieth-century society.

I was too busy to notice, at the time. I had my work to do. I confided to my friend Greta, though. We worked together at the telegraph office.

'Mind you, if Graham's invention works, we'll soon be out of a job,' I said to Greta, between the dots and the dashes.

Greta didn't believe me. 'At the telegraph office? At Central Message Control? No, Alexia, that won't happen. No one ever gets sacked from here.'

'They can get you for unnatural interference with the messages,' I reminded her.

Greta was shocked. 'Alexia, that's never happened! No one would do that! It'd be . . . monstrous!'

'What about redundancy? They can get you on that.'

I shall always remember Greta's patient reply. 'Alexia,' she said, 'morse code and semaphore and messenger boys have been around longer than your brother Graham and his crazy ideas. How's the cat?'

'On the mend.'

'The ice-aeroplane, didn't you say that was another of his latest inventions?'

'Yes, but the telephone is different! I think the telephone is going to work!'

Greta was unconvinced. 'We'd be able to talk to each other without everyone in the teletype room knowing the message.'

'I know, I know.'

'It'll mean the end of twentieth-century society as we know it!'

'No more censors!'

'Shhh!'

'Greta, I just can't get through to Graham. I keep telling him: Graham, the telephone will lead to anarchy.'

'It won't ever happen,' said Greta, as she lectured me on the moral desirability of the Censored State. 'If we were meant to talk to each other down wires then God would have connected us up from birth.'

Graham just kept on working. 'Today the passageway, tomorrow the world,' he announced when I came home one evening.

I found a land-line down the passage and a telephone hook-up in my bedroom. 'Graham, you've gone too far this time,' I bellowed into the phone when it rang. 'Get your inventions out of my room!'

'Alexia, will you step into the next room for a moment?' said Graham on the phone, polite and conscious of the historic moment.

I told him a thing or two. 'Greta says you're a social menace, and I agree with her!' This is a truc account of the first telephone message. You may know part of the story.

First Graham wired up the passage, then he extended the line to every room in the house. Then he wanted more. He wanted to go down the street and clear across Australia, then out into the world.

And he managed to persuade people! Never mind the censors, they soon vanished, once the capitalist entrepreneurs took over. Graham soon had them convinced.

'Gas pipes, water pipes, and telephone pipes!' said Graham, his eyes gleaming and his fingers flying. 'One system, one policy, one universal service!'

'One giant monopoly! And money!' replied the capitalist entrepreneur.

'One grand telephonic system linking each farm to its neighbour, each factory to its central office, each nation to the other!' said Graham, still the visionary.

Remember what it said in the paper? 'We may confidently expect that Mr Bell will give us the means of making voice and spoken words audible through the electric wires to an ear hundreds of miles distant.' It happened.

I tried to warn Graham. 'There may be a few social problems.'

Graham didn't pay attention. 'Nothing a telephone in every house won't fix,' he said.

'There may be a few economic problems,' I warned.

'Show me the economic problem that money won't eliminate!' There was no stopping him.

'Contract distance, contract time!'

'Only a little bit! No one will ever notice!'

'Graham, don't do it! You are going into the unknown.'

'No need to worry,' said Graham, 'I know perfectly well what I'm doing.'

Of course, he got it wrong and we all paid the price. Poor old Greta was one of the first casualties.

'Alexia, what's wrong? My life . . . it's passing so quickly! It seems only yesterday that we worked in Central Control, and now . . . the telegraph! It's vanished!'

I tried my best to distract her. 'Happy birthday darling! Fifty candles on the cake!'

'Then things changed so quickly. The telephone . . . '

'Time's a funny thing.'

Greta blew at the candles. 'Everything started to speed up, and things passed me by, so quickly!'

'There, there, you must have been enjoying yourself.'

'It's not fair! I haven't had time to enjoy myself!'

Of course, Graham could explain it. 'The distinction between past, present and future is only an illusion,' he said.

'It seems real, to me. How can yesterday become tomorrow?'

'If time contracts!'

'That's my problem! What's the solution?'

'I'm working on it,' Graham muttered.

'I can't wait,' said Greta, 'I need it now.'

I discovered that time is more than my perception of it. Time depends on the telephone.

'Nonsense!' you will say. 'Time has been around for simply ages, but the telephone, why, it's only been around for a couple of years!'

'A couple of years? Did you say a couple of years? Why did you say that? I've got you, there!'

'Did I say a couple of years?' you'll say, puzzled. 'Why, of course I meant a hundred years. I don't know why I said a *couple* of years, and with such conviction. It was just a silly mistake.'

Aha, but silly mistakes always mean something! You're confused about the issue, admit it. There's something not quite right about the telephone, something that's hovering on the edge of your comprehension but which can't quite make the break out into your conscious mind. You know, more than you can tell.

Greta and I both noticed something happening. I've worked it out since then.

When Graham got the marketing men interested in his invention, and phones started appearing in every home, time started to speed up for most people. You know how it is, you feel that last year was only yesterday, and that the years of your life are flitting by so quickly. There is a perfectly reasonable explanation. It's because last year was only yesterday, for you, though not for me.

The censors joined the unemployed, the messenger boys went off to two world wars, and wherever the telephone spread, time accelerated in its course. It's only in countries where there are no phones that people still get full value for their lives.

I don't know why it was that Graham and I have not shared the experience. We've either been spared, or punished, for our knowledge. We have stayed outside the onward rush of time. Graham's happy. He thinks he must have invented the elixir of youth in that first experiment. Only the elixir isn't a drug made from gold, or precious herbs, or genetically engineered DNA. The elixir is a unique form of radiation which comes from standing too close to a few tin cans, a thermo-amp, old wires, and a teletype junked in a quite specific way, at a time when Jupiter is on the cusp of Uranus and the moon is in the fourth quarter.

I can't turn the clock back. I can't personally dynamite every telephone in Australia. But I see I shall have to hijack Graham and take him off to Antarctica. He'll come with me willingly enough. Where better to design the ice-aeroplane?

There's a new factor entering into the story. Graham's started to mutter about a new device to contract distance, only this time on a cosmic scale. He can do it, too. The problem with space travel, says Graham, is that space is too big. It's one thing to design a spaceship, but then it takes aeons to get anywhere in it. The stars are too far away. So Graham is working on a device to shrink the galaxy.

Instead of us reaching out to the stars, Graham will have the stars reach down to us.

This is the end. The world has suffered enough.

I, Alexia Bell, being of sound mind, must take my brother Graham to Antarctica, and there build him an ice-hangar for his ice-aeroplanes. I shall lock the door and throw the key from a high window. I make this sacrifice, for you.

Dolphins and Deep Thought

They were on the long trip north along the coast to the place where dolphins came in to swim with people.

It was Ralph's turn to drive. He was doing his best to keep awake. His companions were no help. Ralph tried to interest them in intellectual conversation, but both Susie and Albert fell asleep. Ralph talked on art and life and death and personal immortality, and nature and human nature and, of course, dolphins and their place in the grand scheme of things.

Ralph's words flowed over Susie and Albert, and out of the window and onward to the far reaches of the universe where the cosmic consciousness broods upon the waters and records the fall of feathers from sparrows, and much, much more besides.

Ralph forgave his companions their inertia. They were to be pitied. They were clearly not as tuned as he was to the true pulse of the cosmos.

Beside him, Susie, with Albert in the back seat.

Some time later Albert stirred and grunted and wriggled around so that his knees pressed firmly into Ralph's back. 'We think we've trained those dolphins to come to us. They've really trained us to trek six hundred miles to them.' Albert knows why he's come, but he's not sure where it's going to get him.

It's amazing how quickly a long car trip can bring out the worst in others. Albert finds Ralph's assumption of privileged access to truth increasingly irritating, while Ralph finds Albert a pain in the neck.

Susie copes the best. She's been trying to develop a calm sense of here and now, so she agrees here with Ralph when he talks on art and life, and now with Albert when he talks on science and society. Time flows, words flow, and Susie sits at the calm centre, where words are but short-lived wave disturbances in the air.

Ralph would like to unload Albert, here and now, in the middle of nowhere. But the action would be unworthy. This was part of the problem with his new lifestyle. Thinking nice thoughts, being an empathic individual in tune with the cosmos, it was a strain at times. And eating all that cracked wheat . . .

Albert's tucked up in the back seat with the wheat, the brown rice, the seaweed extract and the puffed millet. Two weeks of whole grain cereal, with Susie and Ralph solicitously watching his mixture of ying and yang, and a diet of high quality food for the spirit, no gross animal products allowed; he's beginning to wonder if he's been wise.

Albert has to have a reason for coming, thinks Ralph. And it's not the same as mine.

Ralph is going into the wilderness to seek purification and salvation among wild animals. Susie's here because here and now seawater bathing with dolphins is the in thing. That's okay for Ralph and Susie. But what will Albert be doing? With his underwater tape recorders and his blip decoding apparatus?

Albert knew that travelling with Ralph and Susie might be tricky, but what else could he do? He's poor now, no job, and the car had to go to pay for the dolphin voice synthesiser. Which he cradles, a model of silicon chip miniaturisation.

Albert's far from his old base, his university, his mathematics and his research grant. The money has come to an end and, as is the way with universities, they have pushed their bird from the nest. Albert has only his ideas to keep him warm. He has found out that out in the world there are people who do not want to talk about mathematics. There are people who expect him to listen while they rabbit on about their children, or the weather, or their life as revealed in the stars.

Albert has gone into the world and he has found it wanting. He has a theory about dolphins and their skills. Putting his theory to the test, that's what's bringing him on the trip with Ralph and Susie. The counterculture is necessary sometimes, for transport. Though Albert is bored with Ralph and the cosmic consciousness, and with Susie and her here and now. 'It's a load of crap, a load of dolphin crap,' he thinks, and shares part of his thoughts with his companions. 'What about dolphin crap?' he asks.

Susie smiles, serene in the here and now, the heat and the car. Ralph shudders.

Albert expands on the problem. 'We'll be swimming in it,' he explains.

There's an intruder in Susie's sense of the here. The future, the swim with dolphins . . . She stops smiling.

Albert pursues the matter more than Ralph and Susie find necessary or desirable. 'Dolphin shit,' says Albert. 'Perhaps it's like goldfish? Thin and stringy and trailing out behind? We'll get tangled up in it. We'll catch worms. Dolphin worms. Liver flukes. Intestinal parasites. I read it somewhere. Fish are full of disease.' Albert's voice is sibilant. There's a hiss in worms, and flukes, and parasites, and disease. Watch it, Ralph and Susie, there's a snake in the Garden of Eden.

Ralph grits his teeth, and meditates on the infinite goodness of nature and nature's own powers of renewal. It's no use. Thoughts of dolphin shit keep intruding.

Albert should be strung up. By the heels. Underwater, with enormous goldfish trailing long threads of luminous brown goo round him, wrapping him up into a tight squirming bundle.

They'd met Albert at a party at college and at first he seemed one of them, an enthusiast for dolphin rights and human liberation through close encounters with the wild. Susie invited him to join them on their trip to the wilderness. Trust Susie to be dopier than usual. Or nicer, intrinsically nicer, treating others as if they were as transparent and guileless as herself. Ralph must continually keep his non-empathic thoughts in control.

Into the wilderness? As they come closer to the bay the dolphins have chosen, Ralph begins to have his doubts. There's the beach along one side of the road, but on the other side there's a row of dusty caravan parks and a tent city strung out in the heat and glare of the midday sun. No trees, no shelter save the sea. There's a Dolphin pub, and a Dolphin fish and chips shop, and a Dolphin T-shirt emporium. They'd been warned of some commercial development. There was even a health food shop: they needn't have carted all that brown rice with them. So many people these days follow an anti-cancer diet.

The street was a disappointment, but the bay itself was as they'd imagined it. Tufts of grass around the edge, a rock platform on the far side, sand and sun and a job of work to be done.

Susie jumped in the water to meet the dolphins. In T-shirt and trousers. That's okay, that's cool. Everyone's dead scared of skin cancer these days.

Albert unpacked his equipment. The voice synthesiser and the microphones and the tapes . . .

Bee-ip-ip, Albert will play to the dolphins. They will listen, and perhaps answer. The trouble will lie, as always, in decoding the response.

Bee-peep-pip, bop-bip-beep. Ralph is sceptical of Albert's plans. Why should Albert expect dolphins to speak in a primitive Morse code?

Susie explains to Albert that dolphins speak to us already. Nonverbally. Without blips or beeps. They come into the bay here to be stroked, to be cuddled. Touch, that's their means of communication. Here and now, immediate gratification.

Susie wants to cuddle a dolphin. Albert wants to teach it calculus. That's the difference between them.

Why calculus? Albert has decided that all previous work with dolphins has got it fundamentally wrong. People have thrown them balls and Frisbees and asked them to play games of fetch and throw.

Dolphins can do it, of course. They can do it, for the ball, the hoop, the Frisbee are objects from the other side. They play with them like a baby plays with bathwater.

Albert has a theory. He knows that the culture of dolphins must be in the head rather than in the hands. They have such a high degree of cortical encephalisation, more impressive than our own. What then do they do with all that brain?

Albert has had a great idea and, like all great discoveries, it's simple, once it's been made. The answer is that dolphins use their brains to think. They're different from us.

Albert knows that the dolphin world is not a world of objects. Why, then, throw them balls? Why start with structures, with objects which are not natural to them?

Let's do it differently, says Albert. Let's start with what the dolphins know, and build on that basis. That way we can move from the known to the unknown. It's more natural.

Let's get into all that cortical encephalisation in the dolphin brain, and get it working for us.

If we've learned that the book of nature is written in the language of mathematics, then it's likely that the dolphins can make the same discovery.

Our world is a world of objects we pile together into structures. Bricks, girders, buildings, cities. Their world is the world of flux, of flow and change, of fluid motion, of fluxions. Fluxions? That's Albert's insight. From Isaac Newton, who invented the calculus and named it fluxions.

Albert will not bother the dolphins with the elementary mathematics of the world of objects. No $2 + 2 = 4$. A child can learn that easily, for the world of blocks stands still for long enough. But the fish which swim past the dolphin's nose are one, or two, or many. The dolphin gets no chance to learn arithmetic. But flow and fluxions and incremental changes, the notion that a line can be regarded as composed of an infinite number of adjacent points, and a surface an infinite number of straight lines, a volume of an infinite number of superposed surfaces: this the dolphins should find a pushover. From that it will be but a short step to the differential calculus, the integral calculus and the functions of a complex variable.

The world is about to become the dolphin's oyster, and it's Albert we'll all have to blame for it, somewhere in the future.

Albert plays with his synthesiser and broadcasts to the dolphins. He translates mathematical patterns into blips, and tapes the dolphins' response. Susie's dolphin listens for a while, but doesn't stay. She prefers Susie and the Frisbee. Her name is Nikki.

Bang goes Albert's theory. Nikki doesn't want to know. Albert keeps trying though. One failure won't deter him. Nikki brings two new dolphins into the bay and up to Albert. The locals comment. The dolphins are named Jason and Tallulah, but not by Albert. Albert cringes at the thought. Jason and Tallulah!

Albert spends his days in the water with Jason and Tallulah. He likes the way they come to swim at his feet. He develops a system of beeps and bee-ip-ips and bips. He finds he doesn't need much sleep. He spends his nights decoding the dolphins' replies. He thinks he's cracked the code, at least enough to begin his plan. He starts with simple differential equations.

'Okay,' says Susie, 'you're teaching the dolphins calculus. What's in it for them?'

Albert doesn't like to think too closely on that one. 'The search after truth,' he responds, stiffly.

'That's what they always say,' says Susie. 'Then they produce the neutron bomb and Frankenstein's monster.'

Still, Albert is grateful to Susie and Ralph. They believe him when he says that his dolphins are learning mathematics. Albert revises his estimates of Ralph's intellect and Susie's cognitive skills.

Albert is happy, for the first time in his life. He likes the life the dolphins lead. Chasing fish and chatting about mathematics. He'd like to join them. Albert wants liberation into their realm of pure thought.

'What about sharks?' asks Ralph. Ralph's pleased that Albert appreciates the true nature of dolphin intelligence, but he's worried that Albert may jump in the deep end.

'Sharks are the least of my problems,' says Albert gloomily. His unpaid bills are beginning to pile up. He plays one bankcard off against the other, but soon the day of reckoning will come, with the Fraud Squad.

Susie worries about Nikki. She's left out of the experiment. She shows no interest in the calculus. 'It's going to limit her choices later in life,' says Susie, 'dropping maths before she's really given it a go.'

'Kids these days!' say Jason and Tallulah. 'Only interested in the here and now. No long-term commitment. To calculus or anything else.'

It's a problem, they agree.

Susie grows thoughtful when Albert tells her about it.

Albert tells the dolphins he'd like to join them. He doesn't tell them about the Fraud Squad. Some concepts don't translate too well past the air/water interface.

The dolphins are prepared to welcome him. 'Sprout some fins,' they tell him.

Albert tells them it's not as easy as it sounds.

'We find it just comes naturally,' they reply.

The joy of his discovery recedes, and he sees his victory has been illusion. If he cannot join them, then all is lost. A life on the ocean wave, with intelligent conversation about mathematics, Albert wants it, and he wants it now.

'I want to be born again,' he tells Susie.

Susie smiles and asks, 'In the usual way?'

'As a dolphin,' he explains.

Susie tells him she can do it. 'Rebirthing,' she says. 'It's easy when you know how.'

Susie will take Albert back to when he began his life's voyage from the womb.

'Here and now?' asks Albert.

Susie is becoming disillusioned with the here and now. She's finding it means she's continually being put upon by other people for their own ends. Here and now. 'Tomorrow,' says Susie, firmly.

Albert is sceptical, that it should be so easy!

The mother Albert desires to find is Tallulah.

Albert tries his best. He goes back, in his mind. He follows Susie's instructions strictly. He slides down the evolutionary scale, back, back, back, to the point of divergence, then forward, forward, past where we are today, onward into the evolutionary future the dolphins have penetrated. He swims up this divergence dreaming of the sea, the sea. He imagines himself dropping from the womb into a warm embracing watery element, soothing him, slapping him on all sides, holding him up, supporting him so that with very little effort he slides to the surface of the water and takes his first breath of air.

He wakens in the present and is disappointed to find, what? Two arms, two legs still? No flippers?

It was worth a try, he confides in Tallulah, but he is near despair. They chat about the functions of a complex variable for a while, but Albert's heart isn't in it.

Jason and Tallulah know he's depressed.

At the end they will wrap him up in sticky brown goo, and he'll be all right. Weeks later, he'll emerge from his cocoon more or less a dolphin, though there'll be a few things wrong. He'll have racing stripes down his sides and there'll be a hiccup in his voice. Albert doesn't mind. The racing stripes make him stand out a little from the common herd. They establish him as a pioneer, as someone who has made culture contact of a truly remarkable kind.

The dolphins, in the end, change Ralph and Susie. Ralph wonders if the cosmic consciousness has been wise. The dolphins may take over.

Susie gives up the here and now, and Ralph. She takes to computers, and to economic forecasting. She knows it's only a matter of time before the dolphins inherit the earth, now they have maths to help them.

Only things will be different then. We've used maths to give us control of matter. For bombs and power stations and microwave cooking.

Dolphins don't want control over matter. That just leads to bigger and better bombs. Dolphins want control over mind instead. Human minds, in particular.

That's why Ralph now works for big business. Mercury pollution of the seas is a good thing, he argues. Pollution is after all a natural spin-off from perfectly reasonable human activities like mining and manufacturing. Something has to dim the dolphin intelligence, or we'll all end up like Albert.

The Bottomless Pit

Once upon a time there will be a girl called Mirium, who will venture forth into the galaxy, and do great deeds.

Mirium will live when the Star Wars are over, and the rule of peace, participation and equity will extend throughout the universe.

She will have no say where she is sent. The rule of peace, participation and equity requires that all will choose right, of their own free will, and no one in their right mind would choose to go to Merinia. Not in the mess it is in.

Mirium will be tricked into going. She will be furious when she finds out. She wants a posting to Axelot, where the glimmerbugs shine and the smugpoobles play. So she carefully places Axelot second on her list and Merinia first. She is a Lateral Thinker.

It is the year they change the system, the year they give everyone their first choice. 'Nobody told me,' wails Mirium, after the event.

Her words cut no ice on the hook-up. The hook-up is the hot line to the Cosmic Consciousness. 'You got what you asked for,' it points out, calmly, with reason and logic on its side.

'You've changed the rules!'

'There's no rule about not changing the rules,' she is told. The Cosmic Consciousness may have messed it up again. Or has it? Who can tell? Mirium will find out on Merinia.

The Cosmic Consciousness is supposed to be an Infinite Intellect with Benevolent Intent, but in practice it doesn't always work that way. And you can't tell it anything! It simply will not listen.

Mirium packs her bags, and says goodbye to family, lovers, friends. It isn't going to be for ever. It's just going to seem like it.

The project on Merinia is a good idea, in principle, but just spot the problems in implementation! Earth was rapidly sinking down the scale in the intergalactic balance of payments stakes, and it is Mirium's task to lead it back to economic recovery, greater efficiency and increased productivity.

The problem is that the universe has enough radioactive waste of its own, and sand, air and water have little bargaining power on an intergalactic scale. Instead Earth has to export its know-how. Lateral thinking.

Lateral thinking is all the rage on Earth – problem solving by the power of brute thought alone. It's where the jobs are, now the mining and agriculture industries have collapsed, thanks to the Merinians.

Earth is exporting education to Merinia.

The problem is, will the Merinians be smart enough to benefit?

This is Mirium's task. She doesn't know where to start.

Merinia is immensely rich because the Merinians devote all their lives to labour. Education should liberate them from boring, degrading, dirty and heavy work. But the Merinians like it that way! They love rolling in the dirt! They take delight in long hours at the coal face, chewing away at the seams! They revel in the repetitive rhythmic pounding of their heads against the rocks as they tunnel underground! At the end of the day they find pure bliss in eliminating from their extremities a number of perfectly formed bricks of brown coal, which they stack in neat piles outside each public lavatory, for the night cart to pick up on its rounds. They enjoy the pleasures of exhaustion to the full.

Plant a Merinian coalbrick, and it goes into an unusual metabolic cycle. The black surface crumbles to a fine yellow dust and minute seeds expand and swell, and if the rainfall is right, the seeds will sprout and within weeks there'll be a fine waving paddock of wheat.

This is the problem. How far should Mirium go, in undermining the activities of a planet as successful as Merinia?

Eternal summer, waving wheat and ecologically sound coalmines. It's one thing to start a revolution if the inhabitants are unhappy, but if they are perfectly well adjusted . . .

Mirium broods amid the alien wheat.

Then she sets out to meet the natives.

'Excuse me,' says Mirium politely, 'but are you a brain in a vat?'

'So you spotted the vat? Nice one.'

'Actually, it was the brain that impressed me.'

The brain in a vat simpers with pleasure. 'Go on, you're having me on,' it says. Then, 'Great vat, this. Custom made. Look!'

Electric pulses career across the oscilloscope. Smoke rises from the rubber. Lights flash. Bells ring.

'Oh!' says Mirium, alarmed. 'Watch out!'

'Nah,' says the brain in a vat, 'only fooling around. It's got automatic cerebral overload and neurone dysfunction cut-off. I was just thinking a great thought. Testing the system.'

'Beats being a brain in a body, then?' asks Mirium, who prefers herself the way she is.

'Any day, any day. Ask any brain in any vat, they'll tell you the same.'

Mirium is not totally convinced, but she will let it pass, for the moment. 'Perhaps you can help me,' she says. She explains her problem. Eternal summer. Waving wheat. Ecologically sound coalmines. The decline in the economy of Earth. The ruinous intergalactic exchange rate.

'What problem? I don't see any problem,' says the brain in a vat, swivelling its sensors round the wheatfields and the coalpiles. Then, 'Have *you* got a problem?' it asks, in a kind and caring fashion. 'You can tell me.'

Mirium persists. 'There is a problem. If you had eyes to see . . . '

The brain in a vat moves into a slight hump. It almost bristles. 'Eyes? Who needs eyes when they can have proprioreceptors like these?'

'Well, what about it? All this . . . coal . . . and wheat?' asks Mirium.

'All my idea,' says the Brain crossly.

'So you're responsible?' Mirium is impressed.

The Brain glows red, then blue, and green fluid flows round its loops. 'You're really rather cute,' says Mirium thoughtfully. 'Tell me how it happened. Tell me everything. I really need to know.'

This is the story the Brain told.

From the point of view of a brain in a vat, the Merinian experiment has been a failure. It has been successful! Let me explain.

Merinia was once a designer planet. To a brain in a vat, the problems of human beings can be simply solved, and on Merinia, some time back, we were given the chance to solve them. Human beings are in a perpetual state of muddle and confusion, at least that's the way it appeared to us. They're muddled about the choices they've been given in life, and they're perpetually tangled up in the way they feel about things. They can't think clearly for two consecutive minutes without wondering whether the cat's been shut in the house for the day, or whether the secretary at the office truly loves them for themselves alone. And as for sexual dimorphism, having male and female a different size and shape, that's been a hideous mistake right from the start. More than anything else it is sexual desire that has stopped human beings devoting their whole lives to unremitting labour.

So the brains in vats stepped in and announced they could solve the problems Merinia once faced. Replace secretaries with word-processors! Mechanise cats! Eliminate the human body! Place the brain in a nice warm comfortable vat with all electrical conveniences! All the problems are solved!

It was hard to get our message across. Only a few Merinians joined us of their own free will. So we had to do something about the rest. Yes, once Merinia was a planet full of messy people, just like any other planet. No particular political system, except whoever won the last revolution stayed in power until the next revolution came along. Tyranny in one country, Democracy in another, Bolshevism, Zimmerwaldism, Nihilism, Imperialism, all in confusing juxtaposition! The planet was a mess!

So the Cosmic Consciousness stepped in some time ago, and gave us brains in vats a free hand in redesigning the planet.

We straightened up the tilt of the planet on its axis, and gave it perpetual summer – enough warmth to remove the tendency to sloth which comes when it's cold outside, and nothing much is growing to farm or hunt or forage for, and people stay later in bed in the mornings and spend the long evenings in front of a large warm fire engaged in idle companionship.

Perpetual summer should have worked. The way everyone groans and shivers and says 'It's cold today' to each other, the way they waste hours of valuable time in idle chatter about the weather – time which could be channelled to socially productive ends!

Perpetual summer should have had something going for it. No, as it turned out. Nobody's thanking us for it now.

And the Merinians! 'You can't change human nature,' that's what they used to say in the old days. Yes, you can! We've proved it! Change nature and human nature goes into a spin!

The secret is simple. Eliminate sexual dimorphism, the fact that male and female look different, and everyone will have so much more time and energy for work! So we put a few chemicals in the water supply, and all new babies from that day on were born androgynous. No more pink for girls, blue for boys! It was grey for everyone and didn't they look just sweet? To anyone with eyes to see. Which of course, I can't. Brains in vats have had to give up most sensorial stimuli for the good life. You spotted that.

Yes, I was there, when it all began. Brains in vats can go on living indefinitely, or until the Cosmic Consciousness pulls the plug, whichever comes first.

And we're responsible for all the mess-up about the coal and the wheat – I'll have to admit it. Sorry! It's just so difficult when you play around with genes! It's hard to hit just exactly the right happy medium! Genes are linked to each other in a variety of quite specific ways, and hit one bit and something else is likely to run amok. Okay, we targeted the sex chromosomes, but somewhere along the way we inadvertently directed some flak at the genes that govern metabolism and, at the end of some trials and errors which are too horrible to remember even for a brain in a vat, we arrived at the perfect Merinian – an androgynous eater of coal!

We brought about androgyny. What does this mean? All males and females identical? No more males and females? Is everyone male? Or female? It is confusing. That's why you need a brain in a vat to sort it out for you.

If a distinction is eliminated, does it still exist?

I look at it this way. Can there be a female mind in a male body? Of course there can't! It would be unnatural! Brains in vats know a thing or two, and the male mind belongs in the male body and vice versa. What you get in an androgynous society is an androgynous mind in an androgynous body! A brain that doesn't spend all its time thinking of glorious soft female warmth . . .

Actually when I had a body I was a man. Now of course, I'm above all feelings of sensuality and softness . . . Actually, I do have these kinds of memories, but I'm not typical of my kind. I think something went wrong in my transition process. To tell the truth, though it isn't quite what they promised, I'm rather happy with my memories, and I wouldn't have it any other way.

Yes, we engineered a few changes in the human body. Female curvaceousness now overlays an endomorphic male bone structure. It means cuddling becomes a bumpier affair, which was all to the good in our plan to eliminate the sex drive as far as possible. Of course, we can't eliminate the sex drive, not totally, you've spotted what you thought was a fatal flaw in our scheme, haven't you? But you can't outsmart a brain in a vat, and we know as well as anyone else that the species has to propagate itself somehow. Our plan was to make the process as efficient and as cost-effective as possible. Which we managed to do.

It's a process called – Merkem.

'Oops!' says the brain. 'Pardon me, I'm coming over strange.'

Mirium notices a few fuses have been blowing.

'I'll just shut down for a while and cool off.' Sparks fly and whistles blow.

'You do that,' soothes Mirium, though she wants to know about the coal and the wheat. There's nothing for it, when a brain starts to blow it starts to blow. She will have to wait.

Mirium looks around at the sun and the sea of waving wheat. If a brain in a vat engineered this mess, then it should be shot. But she lives according to the rule of peace, participation and equity, so shooting was out of the question. But – if a brain in a vat had engineered this mess, then, presumably it could find a way out of it . . . if it could only get its mind off sex for five minutes. It's the same problem, all over the universe.

Where to, next? She spots a machine moving in the next paddock. She gives the slumbering brain in a vat a shove, and they set off together to see what they can find.

'Excuse me,' says Mirium, 'but can you direct me to the nearest Merinian? I've come to meet the natives and so far I've had no luck.'

'Why bother?' answers the machine. It is a Merinian robot-slave. 'They're all the same. Seen one Merinian, seen them all.'

Mirium bristles.

'Call me Picasso,' says the machine. Picasso is a basic black squat box which swivels on rollers. Twelve jointed arms wave independently. Ten eyes are open and observing the best that Merinia has to offer – and finding it wanting. 'Boring eternal summer. Fatuous waving wheat. Boring, boring,' says Picasso. 'Typical of the limited imagination of a brain in a vat.'

The brain recovers, but chooses not to hear. It sits quietly doing some sums. It is trying to work out how to put the tilt back into the axis of the planet, how to bring back winter and slow down growth and induce stay-at-home laziness. It is, after all, a brain with a sense of social responsibility for its creation. Not like the Cosmic Consciousness, which will always go for the cosmic cop-out when the going gets tough. 'It isn't easy,' mutters the brain, but no one is listening.

The robot-slaves of Merinia were designed as the most advanced state of artificial intelligence in the galaxy. Once we thought that we could design a machine, give it a good sense of sight, and then it would do all the boring repetitive dirty work, and we could all retire to a life of freedom and boundless creativity. But mess around with intelligence, human or artificial, and you mess around with some very tricky stuff indeed, and what got engineered into the robot-slave machines of Merinia was a love of beauty.

So robot-slaves like Picasso are useless. They sit around the wheatfields cluttering the place with works of art. They have no intention of being the mugs doing the dirty work that no one else wants to do. They are into personal liberation and their version of the good life.

'You're here to solve their problems?' asks Picasso.

Mirium looks around her with an air of quiet desperation. 'I don't know where to begin,' she confides.

'It's simple, when you know how,' says Picasso kindly.

'You mean you know the answer?' asks Mirium. 'Tell me!'

'Spin straw into gold! Turn coalbricks into works of art!'

'Wow!' says Mirium. 'That's lateral thinking for you!'

Picasso gives a modest smirk. Or would if it could.

Mirium is impressed. Straw into gold! Coalbricks into works of art! Then she spots the fatal flaw.

'Hang on! That solves one problem . . . '

'Yes! No more wheat! No more coalbricks!'

'It solves one problem, but it creates others in its turn.' Life is ever so, thinks Mirium gloomily. Gold instead of wheat! Rembrandts instead of coal! So instead of dumping endless coal and limitless wheat on the intergalactic market, the Merinians will flood it with precious metal and works of art! Earth will be on the skids, only more so!

So there is nothing else for it. Mirium must go forth and find some Merinians, and convince them of the error of their ways. The technological fix is not enough. What must change is human nature – or, in this case, something that is more or less human nature, but not quite.

In many ways the rule of peace, participation and equity has a lot going for it. At least you can move around the galaxy now without being blasted out of the sky. Yes, all the old bang-bang 'Quick, kill the alien before it kills you' stuff is a thing of the past. Once it would have been possible to eliminate the problem by eliminating the Merinians, but now this cannot happen.

And the problem is compounded by the Merinians themselves. They are such nice people, the nicest people you could ever meet anywhere – so nice they make you want to kick them to elicit some kind of grumpy response. But no, Mirium will not resort to physical violence, for that is no longer the name of the game.

Instead she must persuade the Merinians to come to the table of the Intergalactic Central Committee of Management and participate in collective bargaining and democratic decision making.

But as Mirium knows, it's one thing to free the oppressed, if they recognise their oppression. But if they collude in their degradation, if they actively enjoy being put upon, then where can she begin?

Still, there is a glimmer of light. The Cosmic Consciousness has provided the address of an underground movement, a group of Merinians who are seeking to introduce fertiliser farming, mining technology, nuclear power plants and the inefficient use of scarce and dangerous resources. Some of the natives are restless.

Mirium sets out on her way. The brain and Picasso trundle along behind her. They are deep in the debate which occurs whenever a natural intelligence meets an artificial one: 'Which is better, brains or brawn?' Or, in this case, 'Which is better, the human brain or a mechanical brain designed by human beings in full awareness of their own stupidity?'

There will be no easy answer.

In theory, starting a revolution in Merinian attitudes should be simple, Mirium explains to her companions, when she can get them to listen. Point out to everyone the doom which will descend if they don't mend their ways. Then offer the alternatives of new model communities and alternative economic resources. Find a non-useful function for coalbricks and you're away.

Mirium knows that people all over the galaxy are all the same. They've all got persistent attitudes that stand in the way of them ever learning anything. 'We've always done it this way,' they'll say, when asked to mend their wicked ways. Why should it be any different on Merinia?

Okay, so the theory goes. Start with those who realise there's a problem. Then work out from the thin end of the wedge.

Start with the Merinian Revolutionary Front.

But the Merinian Revolutionary Front will not be all it seems.

Mirium finds the Front in a wheatfield. She is introduced – Jerake, then Zev, Xeroff and Blake. They wipe the coaldust from their faces and extend floury hands in friendship.

Mirium is not impressed.

Jerake is short, fat and worried. S/he is pleased to see Mirium, though. 'We thought you were never going to come!' s/he said.

'You've heard of my work?' Mirium cheers up. She has an intergalactic reputation!

Well, no, as it turns out. Jerake has confused her with the delegate from the True Reign of the Spirit Inc. (registered office, Centaurus 5).

Mirium is furious. The Cosmic Consciousness has messed it up again! She explains she is from the Intergalactic Troubleshooting Central Committee for the Economic Reorganisation of Merinia.

There is some confusion and dismay. But mention of the Cosmic Consciousness is enough to bring instant sympathy and understanding. Everyone all over the galaxy knows the trouble it's been. Human beings got what they always wanted, an Infinite Intellect with insight to guide their blundering deliberations. And are they happy with it? Of course not! Instead of the illusion of freedom and participation, they want the real thing! They want to go back to making their own mistakes and now it's too late!

Mirium explains her mission.

The Merinians listen politely, calling on the Brain to translate some of the tricky bits. But they get her message and she gets theirs, and they begin to see some common ground. Jerake is the leader of a breakaway group who are fed up with unremitting labour. They plan to drop out into a life of meditation and contemplation. Their minds are set on a higher wavelength, far away from the business of soft technology and ecologically sound food production. They want to liberate the Merinian mind, so the body will drop away and the realm of the true Spirit will be attained!

It will solve the balance of payments problem, but Mirium is not convinced. She points out, calmly, with reason and logic on her side, that no one in the galaxy has succeeded in pulling off the True Reign of the Spirit yet, and now we all know about the Cosmic Consciousness no one anywhere has any illusions about someone, somewhere having all the answers to our problems.

Zev tries his/her best to reassure her. 'The Centaurans are helping us! They're working on our problem, from afar!'

'The Centaurans?' says Mirium. 'From afar? Why can't they come here, if they're free as the Spirit?'

'They're waiting for a security clearance.' Jerake passes a floury hand over a coal-streaked brow. 'Something to do with a small tax problem.'

Mirium persists. 'Why not become a brain in a vat? What's the difference? Join the club.' They all look at the brain.

The brain preens itself. Everyone sighs.

'Thank you, no, I don't think so, not for the moment,' they say.

'It's all a question of . . . well, mobility,' Blake explains. 'In a state of bliss, we'll be able to travel freely through the ether! We'll be able to ride the wings of the morning, and live the untrammelled life of the spirit!'

'Except for security visas and exit clearances,' Mirium says to herself.

'A brain in a vat, yes, it leads the life of the intellect, but it has its limitations, at least as we see them. It's stuck in the same place all the time . . . '

'So are the Centaurans,' Mirium murmurs.

' . . . it's stuck in the same vat all the time, it's reliant on others to change the nutrient broths and monitor the electrical print-outs. A brain in a vat has the life of the intellect. But we want more. We want the life of the Spirit.'

'The Centaurans know the way. They used to be physical like us, but look at them now!'

'Actually, you can't look at them now, they're invisible, and . . . '

'And they're only asking half a million Merinian dollars!'

Mirium listens and asks, 'For the True Reign of the Spirit? For everyone on the planet?'

'Yes!' they all chorus. 'It's a steal at the price!'

Eliminate the Merinian problem by eliminating the Merinians! But peacefully, and because they want to go! It sounds too good to be true, to Mirium. 'Let's get this one straight,' she says. 'They want you to pay them money to translate the inhabitants of the planet to a state of ethereal bliss?'

'That's where you come in,' the Merinians tell Mirium.

Mirium is surprised to hear it.

'You've brought the money?' they ask.

'What money?'

'The half-million Merinian dollars.'

'I haven't got any money!' says Mirium. 'I'm just the Lateral Thinker round here.'

'No money?' There are sighs all round. Jerake looks more worried than ever. 'I've already made them the offer. I said I'd bring it. The half-million.'

'If the Centaurans can't come to us . . . '

'We were planning to send Jerake to them.'

'With the money . . . ' says Mirium thoughtfully. It might be the usual message, true contemplation of the Spirit stuff, but as usual the Path must be strewn with dollars first.

'I thought the Merinians were rich,' says Mirium. 'Isn't that the problem? That you've got most of the money in the galaxy? And nobody else has any? Where does all the money go?' Mirium has set her companions thinking, but they can't come up with the answer.

No one has ever asked them the question.

Mirium is puzzled. If Merinia is ruining the economy of the galaxy, then they must have something to show for it. Wealth, or a high standard of living, or conspicuous consumption of an outstanding order of magnitude. But the Merinians lived simple lives of work and sleep. They had enough to eat, the best high roughage and low fat diet, and plenty of carboniferous material for which their digestive tracts were ideally suited. When she thought about it, there was no vulgar show of wealth to be seen anywhere on the planet!

What is happening? How can she find out?

Mirium confers with Jerake and the brain and the robot-slave Picasso. They are impressed by the question she has thought to ask.

Where does all the money go?

They go to the nearest hook-up and they ask the Cosmic Consciousness.

Of course it knows the answer. The Cosmic Consciousness can be a colossal pain in the neck. 'The money?' it says. 'Of course I know where it is!'

'Why didn't you tell us?'

'Because you didn't ask,' it says. An Infinite Intellect is no solution to anyone's problems. It may be the One Who Should Know All, but it is often cagey about parting with its information.

'Where is it then?'

'In the bottomless pit,' it replies.

'The bottomless pit – how do we get there?'

'Across the Plains of Sommer, around the Mountains of the Moon, to the South-seeking Pole of Merinia. Then dig.'

'Thanks a million.'

'Don't mention it,' smirks the Cosmic Consciousness, signing itself over and out.

Hey-ho for the Plains of Sommer and the Mountains of the Moon!

Where does all the money go? At the South-seeking Pole of Merinia, far across the Plains of Sommer and the Mountains of the Moon, space shuttles land and discharge their cargo of money. It is an automated process. Doors open according to a predetermined programme, and the money, in all shapes and sizes, falls into an almost bottomless pit. That's where all the money goes. Into a hole in the ground.

Why does this happen? On Merinia, they've always done it this way.

After all, what use will money be to a happy well-integrated community like Merinia? Where all the food they need is supplied in the form of flour and carbon? Where the sun shines all the time, and money is not needed for central heating and cocktail dresses and gourmet food and jacuzzis and general frivolity?

It makes a certain kind of sense. But it's ruining the galaxy.

Mirium has come to be fond of her companions. They are so eager to help in the intergalactic crisis! They will all come with her to show her the way!

And they are so busy. The brain in a vat continues with its computations. 'Nearly there,' it gasps now and then, when it can be roused. 'Nearly there! Nearly got the tilt back in the axis! Just a little! To bring back winter, you know, the time when it gets cold, and the wheat stops sprouting, and the days grow short, and everyone cuddles up nice and warm in front of a glowing fire, and it's so pleasant and comfortable and sensuous and delicious . . . '

The robot-slave Picasso is doing its bit. As it trundles along behind them, chaff goes in one end of its rollers and pure gold threads come out the other side. These are automatically wound into bales and left neatly stacked on the edges of the wheatfields. When they rest for lunch, Picasso stays on the go, busily fusing coalbricks into works of art. Giant fossilised trees marking their passage across the Plains of Sommer.

They are doing their best and Mirium is proud of them. With friends like these, the universe is in good hands.

Of course, trekking to the South Pole was easy going, on a planet like Merinia. The poles have the same climate as everywhere else. It's not like Earth, with the trek through the blizzard with dog packs and pony teams and frost-bitten fingers and toes. There was plenty of food for Jerake in the coalmines and the wheatfields, and for Mirium it was dehydrated glimmerbugs and liquefied smugpoobles, as usual.

Mirium is glad of the company, and talks of the old days on Earth, and the terrible hardship and the extremities of cold endured by Scott and Amundsen and Edgeworth David on their trips southward to the

Pole. How they ate seal and hoosh and pemmican and pony fricassee, but never each other, for getting there first was an activity for gentlemen, and dying in the attempt was the stuff from which heroes were made.

'Up and down the glaciers . . . ' says Mirium, while Jerake listens politely and now and then asks the brain to translate the tricky bits. 'Frozen socks?' queries Jcrake, and the brain pauses in its calculations to provide the Merinian equivalent.

'Any minute,' gasps the brain. 'Nearly got the answer, give me another week!' No one pays it any attention, until the planet starts to wobble under their feet.

'Help!' and 'Stop that brain!' and 'It's done enough to mess up this planet as it is!' Cries come from all around. But the planet is tilting and night is falling and it's only four o'clock in the afternoon! And it's getting cold!

'Switch that brain off,' they cry, but it is too late.

So they trudge on through the gathering gloom.

'Merkem,' says Jerake, stopping in his tracks.

'Merkem,' say his followers, getting excited.

'Help!' says the brain in a vat and the machine Picasso. 'This is madness! Don't do it! Not here and now! Not in front of the children!'

'It's our one and only chance,' the Merinians plead. 'It's the one day of the year!'

'Not when the future of the galaxy is in your hands, and night is falling and . . . it's starting to snow!'

But fundamental biological urges will out, and Merkemisation proceeds, at its own pace, as it will. Merkem is the way they reproduce the species on Merinia.

'It will happen on the day we reach the Pole.' The Merinians are happy, but everyone else is beginning to wonder if they have been entirely wise. It is getting colder and darker, and the Merinians are getting wilder and wilder.

Each day they are a little closer to the goal. Each day the magnetic needle points a little more to the vertical. Each day the Merinians change in ways that amaze their fellow travellers. Beards become longer, breasts become more pronounced, excitement rises and voices break.

Meanwhile Picasso is proving a machine with a heart of gold. Literally. It spins wheat into gold, and gold thread into cloaks which keep out the cold and serve to disguise the more outrageous changes taking place in the Merinian anatomy. For some of the Merinians are becoming women, while others are becoming men, and the day of the Pole is fast approaching!

Jerake now has a deep bass voice. He has taken to dogging Mirium's footsteps and she is trying to remember all she has ever read about inter-species sexuality. It's terrible how vital facts will slip the mind at moments of crisis, and she cannot for the life of her remember whether she has had her protective shots. Or what precisely they will protect her from.

So they trudge on.

Then they see it! The shuttle is coming in to land!

It's true! There is a giant money rocket, which crosses the galaxy, hopping from solar system to solar system, collecting money from all and offloading it on Merinia. Doors open on the surface of the planet and the money falls from the rocket into the pit. It's all done by remote control. The pit is covered by a shining plate of artificial wheat, but once you know it's there, the outlines of the opening are easy enough to see.

It's the bottomless pit! And it's full of money!

The shuttle departs and they run forward to look down.

Then the Merinians start to come over strange. It never rains but it pours, says the brain in a vat, preparing to switch itself off and lie doggo for the duration.

Then, 'The Centaurans! They've come!' says Jerake.

They are surrounded by a rushing whirling wind. Voices of welcome fill their ears. Jerake turns his eyes to the hills and Mirium can relax.

'The money,' the Spirit voices whisper. 'You've got the money? We want it now.'

'Whatever happened to your small tax problems?' asks Mirium tersely.

'When we heard you couldn't make it to us . . . '

'We came to you.' The Centaurans come in the true spirit of inter-galactic brotherly love. And for the money.

So they solve Mirium's problems and she is grateful. They give Jerake a shot of Bliss and he shimmers faintly in the pale light of the Pole with the pleasure of it all.

'The money?' The heavenly voices are insistent.

'There's plenty of money in the pit,' says Jerake, 'but how will you get it out?' He is growing paler and more translucent. And grinning wildly with the pleasure of it all.

'Nothing to it,' say the Spirits, and they float down into the abyss. In no time at all they clean out all the money. They transform it into the spiritual realm, as fast as lightning strikes, or dreams flee the waking mind. All the money! All gone!

And the bottomless pit is empty.

Jerake is a hazy semi-transparent glow. He is going to join the realm of the Spirit. Mirium has to tell him her news fast. 'I've got it!' she yells. 'I've got the answer. It's in the bottomless pit!'

Then there is the sound of a mighty roaring wind and Mirium is lifted up into the air with a swoop and a flourish. 'Join me!' calls the voice of Jerake through the ether.

'No. Listen, Jerake. I have the answer! The answer to the problems of Merinia!'

Mirium flies on the wings of the morning, with the joy of discovery in her heart. 'Don't you see? We won't have to change the Merinians! Or convert them all to the Pure Reign of the Spirit! Or bring them education that they do not want, and nuclear technology and giant windmills that they do not need! All we have to do is . . . give them the bottomless pit!'

The wind that was Jerake gives a swoop and a dive, and throws Mirium into the air and catches her again.

Yes! The Merinians don't have to sell their wheat and coal to the galaxy for money! Not when they've got a bottomless pit! All they need to do is shovel the coal and the wheat into the pit! Cut out the middle man and save the intergalactic economy!

So the Cosmic Consciousness was right, after all. Merinia needed Mirium. Her intelligence is not up to the high standard set by natural and artificial brains in vats or out of them. But she has the capacity to see what others miss. The blindingly obvious.

So the day of Merkem rolls on its way. Spiritual ravishment leaves the other kind for dead, thinks Mirium, as she flies with Jerake for a day and a night.

Then she leaves at last for Axelot, where the glimmerbugs shine and the smugpoobles play.

Trickster

The ancient dried out Lake Mungo in western New South Wales and Mungo Woman who was found there are now part of the international archaeological dictionary. Her cremation established human occupation in Australia at at least 40,000 years, at a time when the Neanderthal Man was still in Europe. Not only that, but the Aboriginals at Lake Mungo were modern people, and they left behind evidence of a belief in an after-life, a kind of Dreaming.

Kirsten Garratt, *From Mungo to Makaratta*

'What's it all for?' Alicia asked, the day she started work. The row of fossil skulls marched along the edge of the table, ranged in order from the most gracile at one end, to the most rugged at the other.

'It's called human research,' she was told. 'It's the science of human nature.'

Alicia had her doubts right from the start, but she kept them to herself.

She was shown around the skull room. The table with the row of skulls stood in the centre. The rest of the bones were sorted into white boxes, each neatly labelled with names – ribs, humerus, ulna. They stood in stacks along the walls. Filing cabinets were filled with casts and reconstructions of missing pieces of bone. So much hard work, so much material, collected, collated and reconstructed from a belief in the value of human research.

'You'll soon get used to it here,' she was told. 'It's a job, like any other.'

'That's what I thought,' said Alicia, glowing with life and love in the house of bones.

Alicia is formally introduced. 'This is the skull from Cow Swamp.' The skull from Cow Swamp sits in a pool of light, fixed upright to a frame.

Alicia inclines her head.

'And this is the skull from Keilor.' Alicia is suitably grave. One must respect the dead.

'This is the skull from Green's Bush.' The introductions continue. Alicia wonders how she will remember it all.

'It's easy, once you know how,' says Rosie. She's worked there for years. Rosie Byrne knows her way round the skull room.

'Everything is,' murmurs Alicia.

Alicia learns the ways of the skull room. There are frequent arguments, for a start.

'What's it all for?' Alicia asks her new colleagues, those who could speak.

'It's so we know where we're going, that we have to find out where we've been.' Plowright liked his origins clear, and his future predictable.

'We all want to know where we're going. We just disagree about where we've come from,' Rosie explains to Alicia.

Alicia listens and learns.

'It's who we've come from,' says Anthony Torok.

Torok finds the bones a problem.

For Rosie Byrne, it was easy. The first man was a woman.

Torok disagrees. 'What makes you so sure?' he asks.

'What makes you so sure it's not?' she replies.

Her colleagues think she's perverse.

Torok doubts whether the beginnings of culture can be traced to any one individual with an exceptionally prominent brow. 'You can't say, here civilisation begins, here in Cow Swamp, just because we've got a few bits and pieces of bone to play around with.'

'It's obvious, once you think of it,' says Rosie to Alicia. The women work together in the skull room, calipers in hand and computers at the ready. 'What's wrong is the idea. What's wrong is the ape man.'

'It's obvious, once you think of it,' says Anthony Torok. 'What's wrong are the bones. The bones didn't change the world. The world changed the bones, just once, at one time, at one place.'

'That place is Europe,' says James Plowright.

'That place is Africa,' says Anthony Torok.

'That place is Melbourne,' says Rosie Byrne. 'Cow Swamp, to be precise. There, *homo* became *sapiens*, saw the light, and then took off for Europe.'

At night in the skull room the bones rearrange themselves, a little, not much. The indentations in the skull from Cow Swamp deepen. The orbital ridges thicken. Scratches in the teeth enamel sink in, just a fraction.

Soon there will be a new theory of the origins of the human race.

The workers in the skull room assume the bones remain the same and it is their theories which change. But that is not the case.

The bones know. It amuses them.

'There's always a margin of error,' say the scientists. But they mean a margin of error for them. They do not consider that it might be the skull which is playing fast and loose with their measurements.

Scientific truth is only relative, and the fact that scientific truth is only relative is the only thing that really is true. Truly? Yes, truth is never the whole truth, and that is the name of the game.

It doesn't matter, provided the skull plays fair. But the skull from Cow Swamp never learned the rules.

Rosie Byrne is increasingly delighted with the skull's activities. She sees teeth which are worn in a particular manner.

'Look,' she says to her colleagues. 'It's the way the teeth are worn.'

'Yeah,' they say. They have their own work to do.

'I mean, it's the way the teeth aren't worn.' Rosie was all for the search after truth.

The skull sits in its frame, unblinking.

'The skull from Cow Swamp, it's a woman.'

Her colleagues have heard it all before.

The first man was a woman? The skull was buggered it if knew.

The workers in the skull room believe the bones are legitimate enough. It is the claims made for them that are preposterous.

For the skull all claims for legitimacy are relative. That's okay. It knows it's fiddling the evidence.

For the workers, there is the search after truth.

For the skull, there is the element of trickery. A forgery may, after all, be a form of art and the end of art is to provide us with something from which we can learn a great deal.

The skull could promise them that.

Alicia dreams of life and love.

Rosie dreams of fame. She's sometimes worried though. What if she's right, but she gives the wrong reason?

Nobody's perfect.

The Fall of Man: that's a metaphor for the burden of animal instincts that survives as a leftover from the past. So that we may know instinctively that we are right, though reason cannot tell us why. In this corruption may lie our intuitive strength, or just corruption pure and simple. Inside the man of reason, there may lurk the fraud. Inside each skull there lurks the trickster.

But that's the tricky part. How can a skull be said to deceive?

'Such teeth,' said Rosie Byrne when she next saw them. 'Nice and unworn, a woman's teeth. It's a cultural thing,' she explained to her colleagues. 'The men chew kangaroo tendons and their teeth get worn in a quite distinctive way.'

Such teeth, all the better to eat you with, said Pleistocene man to Pleistocene marsupial. The skull knew more than it could tell.

Plowright kept his thoughts steady. He wasn't going to rewrite the entire prehistory of Australia because of a few new ideas. He was, after all, the boss. He had to keep the funds rolling in.

Rosie broods. Men of reason and men of business speak much the same language. Both after all, want profit, though one speaks of profit in the search for gold, the other of gain in the search after truth. There can be no loss in the search for knowledge, that's one advantage. For even the wrong question, correctly answered, can tell us something, even if it tells us we were wrong in the first place. That is, all told, a gain, for the worker has gained some credit. Though of course she gains more if she asks the right question and receives the right reply.

In the skull room there is the goal of knowledge, and the goal of glory. In the search after truth, there may be some glory, but little truth; there may be some credit, though a loss is recorded.

Some say that the goal 'to know' serves only the function of rhetoric, that what matters is only the cycle of rewards and advances. But that is a cynical viewpoint.

The skull changes, doing it slowly, and new measurements do not agree with the old.

'It's an unacceptable margin of error,' Rosie is told.

She is puzzled, but cheerfully accepts criticism in the spirit in which it is intended. Or she says she does, while gritting her teeth and snarling at Alicia.

Oh, the tyranny of the skull.

Anthony Torok smiles and does not overtly sneer.

Alicia is reading the papers, searching for another job.

In every court, there is a jester. In every circus, there is a clown. In every tribe, there is a trickster.

It buggers up the search after truth no end.

Rosie never gets to publish her discovery.

There is a court case, and the bones must be returned to the place they came from.

The bones are gathered up for cremation. They are taken to a river bank.

We must respect the dead. We must burn the bones.

They are burned according to old rites.

The workers in the skull room are liberated from the tyranny of the bones. Only they do not know it.

Rosie Byrne doesn't see it that way. She weeps for the end of knowledge. Then she dries her tears.

'It was a good job, while it lasted,' says Alicia.

James Plowright finds a congenial job in the public service, and Anthony Torok joins a university.

The bones are going. The bones are gone.

Nothing remains.

At the cremation site, dust and ashes move, in a purposeful fashion.

They form new shapes. Soon there will be new games played on new-comers to the search after truth.

There will be campfire sites, and middens.

There will be radio-carbon dating and spectroscopic analysis.

What does it matter, in the end? The activity called problem solving is all. The results matter less. Every problem which is solved will raise others in its turn, and so the search after truth will go on, indefinitely, into the future.

The Sea-Serpent of Sandy Cape

'When I saw the sea-serpent,' Miss Lovell wrote with strong black strokes, 'I confess I was not prepared for it. The children, Jemima, Jessie and Robert, saw it first and they came running up the sandhill calling for me to come. I was admiring the stillness of the sea and the beauty of the day.'

'What do you think?' Dr Ramsay asked his companion.

'Folderol,' McIntosh replied.

'There's a consistency there, with other accounts . . . '

'Which is why these people see things in the first place.' McIntosh was interested in the story, but not in the sea-serpent.

'The platypus exists, though, and who'd have believed it?'

'Nobody, and with reason.'

'My point precisely.'

'No, my point.'

'There's the great deep out there, and hidden places, hidden forces . . . '

'And on dry land, there's human folly.' McIntosh can't believe it's his rational friend who is speaking. 'Read the letter again. It's a tall story, nothing more.'

Ramsay continued with Miss Lovell's story.

'I went to the water's edge and there I saw a huge animal, of a most pleasant and gentle demeanour. It lay quietly, its long neck rising from the water. The skin was glossy, smooth as an egg and shiny as silvery-grey satin. The head was snake-like, but the neck disappeared into a tough velvety carapace, like a turtle's, ridged with a pattern of small grey squares. The other odd thing was its tail, which I saw only when it dipped its head under the water. It was long, forked at the end and covered with scales as large as a thumbnail, scales of a rich chocolate brown, a colour so different from the rest of the animal, and the tail so distant from it, that at first I thought there were two quite distinct animals. We watched from the shore for fifteen minutes and then the two halves of the creature moved as one and, in the time it took me to take one breath, the creature disappeared, emerging again, just once, far out to sea where the steamers pass.'

'Not one, but two monsters! Nature is prodigal!'

'It's consistent with Poppopidian. The sea-serpent appears only when the water is flat and the weather is clear.'

Poppopidian compiled a record of sightings back in 1820, when he wrote *The Natural History of Norway*. Why do records of sea-serpents exist, if sea-serpents do not?

'According to Poppopidian, Norway abounds in sea-monsters.'

'Norway abounds with people who say they've seen sea-monsters. It's not quite the same thing, Ramsay.'

'We must keep an open mind. If the sea-serpent of Sandy Cape exists, then the British Museum wants it and they'll pay for it.'

That's the very best reason for keeping an open mind and it keeps Ramsay reading.

'Round here, the local name is Moha Moha. They say it has four feet, like an alligator, and can walk on land. The creature did not choose to reveal its feet to me, although I tried to see them through the water, so I make no claim about the feet, but Robert tells me he saw them, the Monday previous.'

'The testimony of children and women . . . ' McIntosh is sceptical.

Ramsay read on:

'We, the undersigned, saw the Moha Moha making for the shore of Sandy Cape on the eighth day of June in the year of 1890. James Alsbury, First Assistant, Sandy Cape Lighthouse; William Lees, Third Assistant, Sandy Cape Lighthouse; Mrs Lees; Jemima Alsbury, Jessie Alsbury, daughters of James Alsbury; Robert (his mark); Rebecca Lovell, Schoolmistress, Sandy Cape Lighthouse Community.'

'Where was the second lighthouse keeper, I'd like to know?' grumbled McIntosh. He was impressed in spite of himself. They considered it worth the trip from Brisbane up to Sandy Cape. For Ramsay there could be a prize for biology, and as for McIntosh, he declared himself always available to record human folly in its many forms.

The mangrove swamp was a place of rare beauty, but Miss Lovell was the only one who saw it. Her mangrove sketches were singular, though whoever took delight in them must like mud and black twisted roots and seedpods sprouting and pippis peeping half-in, half-out of the mud-flat. Her paintings were more traditional. Here's a delicate prawn, clear white, with pink translucent spots, a pen and wash affair, and in the background the blue and green tentacles on the anemone in which the prawn resides and lives protected and commensal with its host.

Her ink drawings were not . . . nice. That was the judgment of Mrs Lees. Though since the coming of the Moha Moha, Mrs Lees had a new respect for Miss Lovell and her biological interests. A new alliance has been forged. For Miss Lovell's report has brought many visitors to Sandy Cape, and Mrs Lees gives them teas, scones and jam for sixpence.

'Tell me, Miss Lovell, about the habits of sea-serpents,' said Mrs Lees, wiping her hands on her apron and thinking of scones and jam. A knowledge of natural history had its uses.

'What is the definition of a sea-serpent? It is unmysterious. A sea-serpent is merely an elongate marine creature of an apparently unknown species, nothing more,' Miss Lovell explained.

'Like the monster in Loch Ness?' Mrs Lees must get back to her work, but she needed to sort out a few facts first.

Miss Lovell set her straight. 'The monster from Loch Ness is not a sea-serpent. It is more properly a lake monster and, as such, is not to be confused with our own Barrier Reef product.'

'It's truly a marvel,' said Mrs Lees, and she went back to the lighthouse to count her money.

'Who is being hysterical? I'm not being hysterical,' said Miss Lovell. She frowned at McIntosh when he ventured the suggestion. 'Tell me one thing, Mr McIntosh. If sea-serpents do not exist, why have you travelled so far? To see something which isn't there?' She paid no attention when McIntosh explained his theory of perceptual contagion. 'It's like this,' he said. 'First one person sees something, then another falls victim to suggestion, and then another, for there is by then the expectation created, the stage is set and the image is already in the mind. The sea-serpent does not have to be out there, in the real world.'

Miss Lovell gave all her attention to Dr Ramsay. 'I expect you will want to see the beach?' she asked, and she took the two men to the water. Dismissively, to McIntosh, she said, over a shoulder, 'If I say I have seen a sea-serpent, Mr McIntosh, rest assured, it is the case.'

It was hot and sticky and the air hummed with the sounds of insect life. Sandflies found difficulty in biting Miss Lovell, for she was swathed in clothes from neck to ankle. She was an observer of nature, not a participant in the ritual of predator and prey. The men were dressed as all naturalists should dress, when confronting the rigours of the Queensland climate. Each wore a sensible solar topee, insulated at the top with a layer of air, thus guarding against the ever-present danger of sunstroke and consequential brain-fever. Sensible jackets, of course, and high collars, a cravat each, long woollen trousers and button shoes.

The insect life retired, defeated.

The tide was out, Miss Lovell explained, and the shallow lagoon they saw before them was not there the day the sea-serpent came. Ramsay busied himself with questions on length, height, weight and colour, and speed of swimming: all that could be numbered, weighed and measured.

'Size, length and weight, what does it matter?' McIntosh found the whole thing farcical.

Ramsay and Miss Lovell talk earnestly about the tail. 'Forked, you say?' asked Ramsay. 'That would be atypical. Alligators don't have forked tails, nor do turtles.'

Miss Lovell was generous. 'Perhaps the tail was paddle-shaped,' she conceded. 'With a large bite taken out of the middle, by some shark, or some creature similar to itself. That's what Jemima said when she saw it and she's a sharp child.'

'I'll talk to her later,' Ramsay promised. He was in his element, with sand, sun and water, and a job to be done.

On the beach, Ramsay came to the point. 'The British Museum promises one hundred pounds for the complete animal, fifty for part and a fair price for the head and neck, sun-dried.'

Miss Lovell sighed: 'Demand for the Moha Moha is likely to exceed supply. I'll see what I can do, but you understand I cannot promise delivery.'

So up in the lighthouse, Billy Lees kept his eyes open for the Moha Moha. If you see a sea-serpent catch it quickly, that's the point of this tale. Do not be taken in by its soulful eyes or its gentle nature. It may have a peaceable disposition, but that won't bring in one hundred pounds, sun-dried.

Miss Lovell imposed some conditions on her visitors. 'It is a sea-serpent of a gentle disposition. I do not wish it to be cut up for soup.'

'Of course not,' said Ramsay. 'It will be cut up for science.'

Ramsay was careful. One must keep an open mind, but it should not be a totally vacant one. Miss Lovell's testimony, he decided, could not be disregarded. She had seen something quite remarkable. For sea-serpent sightings, it is ordinary people on whom we must rely, people who are there when the extra-ordinary happens, because they are going about their daily business. Miss Lovell will go out daily and walk along the beach, for she finds thrill enough in the ordinary, in the sea-snake sloughing its gun-metal skin or the bêche-de-mer ejecting its own intestines. She does not need the extra-ordinary for her purposes. That is why she may find it.

They lay in wait for the Moha Moha but, to tell the truth, nobody quite knew how to set about it. The lighthouse keepers had the advantage, but they couldn't spend all day looking out of their octagonal windows. McIntosh didn't try very hard. He spent his time on the beach looking in the wrong direction, up the sandhill and over to the headland, observing the local birds out on Break-Sea Spit, and he did it on purpose. The children were always down on the beach, but they made inconsistent observers. Visitors came, and watched and picnicked, and did not seem to worry much when after a day of waiting, nothing had happened.

McIntosh found the human material for his study increasingly tedious. The people of Sandy Cape were so convinced of their rightness and so resistant to his suggestions of delusion that he was beginning to wonder if it wasn't a case of outright fraud. 'They're all in it together,' he told himself. For what? For the money? Tea and scones will hardly make Mrs Lees her fortune, though it served to make a dull life busy. Miss Lovell? She has her reputation to consider, as schoolmistress of Sandy Cape. In whose interests would deception be?

'Perceptual contagion?' murmured McIntosh, but with increasing doubt. 'Active collusion, more like it.' He took himself off for afternoon tea with Mrs Lees. His life at Sandy Cape had settled into a routine.

One day they found a deep footprint, of an animal unknown at Sandy Cape. A curious footprint, for it was strange, really, to find just one, at the shore line, at dawn, with the tide advancing up the beach towards it. The black boy Robert found it and he came running up to the lighthouse to wake the visitors.

It worried Ramsay a little, he had to confess, when he came down, with calipers and plaster of Paris and notebook in hand. A solitary footprint? Ramsay began to wonder whether perhaps his friend McIntosh might be right after all, that he was the victim of a practical joke.

'Jemima, Jessie, tell me, have you ever heard the story of Robinson Crusoe?' he asked them casually, when he could get them away from the others. Jemima and Jessie chatter and giggle, and look at the footprint, and look away again, and say, yes, they know the story.

'I thought you might,' said Ramsay grimly.

The children seem so wide-eyed and innocent, they must be guilty.

Ramsay took the measurements and prepared the plaster of Paris, but the joy had suddenly gone out of his work. Faking a footprint, that'd be quite an easy thing to do. Especially one which will soon disappear with the tide. Ramsay was an expert on fossil fish, not on saurian footprints. Anyone could do it. There was Robert, he'd have some clues about the limits of the possible. It was Robert who told them the local stories of the Moha Moha in the first place. Robert wouldn't know of Robinson Crusoe, but someone else could have put him up to it. Miss Lovell? He couldn't believe it. James Alsbury, pillar of lighthouse keeper rectitude and puritan morality? Again, it strained the imagination. Of course, thought Ramsay, the person we least suspect is the one who's likely to be the most to blame, when the story comes out in the end. The more he examined the people around him, the more they all looked far too innocent. It could turn out to be, in the end, a case of collusion against him, against science and against morality.

The more Ramsay tried to analyse the footprint, the less convincing it seemed.

Round him the residents of Sandy Cape buzzed like sandflies. They chattered about the position of the animal and its posture. It was heading in the direction of the water, they decided. Hardly surprising, thought Ramsay. The toes pointed towards the sea. And where were the other footprints? Why just one? Ramsay caught the eye of McIntosh and was troubled.

Miss Lovell displayed the depth of the indentation, and the shape of the toes. Toes? Talons? Claws? There was an element of each. All it needed to see them was a little imagination, as all theory and its relation to practice must require.

Ramsay asked McIntosh his opinion, though he thought he knew it already.

'More collusion,' replied McIntosh. But who is fooling who? McIntosh knew he knew some of the answers, for he had faked the footprint. Rather clever that, he's proud of his capacity to present so much excitement to the Sandy Cape community. All it took was an afternoon, a horseshoe, some plaster of Paris and his own undoubted skills in sculpture. He's been leaving fake footprints around for a week, but nobody's noticed till now.

McIntosh wants his forgery to flush the real villains. He thinks that the discovery of a second fraud will tell those who perpetrated the first fraud that someone is on to them.

If the first announcement was a fraud, that is.

He could be wrong, of course, for as the days went by, the footprint only seemed to him to be confirming the residents of Sandy Cape in their delusions. More and more, McIntosh decided at last, he must return to his notion of perceptual contagion. These people are not in active collusion. They have all deceived themselves. That he has come to this conclusion by means of deception does not worry him at all. In the search after truth, the ends must justify the means.

The people of Sandy Cape are in a state of perceptual readiness. They want to see the sea-serpent.

'It never existed in the first place. It was a figment of the imagination,' said McIntosh. He was going home. He'd talked to everyone and had his theory safe and sound. They were all deluded and he was the only person at Sandy Cape with true clarity of vision. 'A true case of perceptual contagion,' he'll call it, and he'll write it up for the medical journals.

When McIntosh said, 'Sea-serpents do not exist,' he was surely helping to create the conditions under which sea-serpents will not exist. For if we go around saying that the sea-serpent is a mythical beast, then people will not tell when they think they have seen one. They will be scared of being thought deluded or drunk, or both.

They spent one last night on the beach, observing. Down they went with hurricane lamps and rugs and scones and jam, prepared to make a scientific event or a social occasion of it. McIntosh brought his folding telescope and his stand, and set it up to look at the stars: anything but the sea. Ramsay had his tape-measure, his calipers and his optimism.

Ramsay and Miss Lovell spent some time discussing the naming of the sea-serpent. Moha Moha will not do, they decided, for though it was euphonious, it had the ring of the arbitrary about it. 'It's half saurian, half turtle. *Chelosaurus*, will that do? *Chelosaurus Lovelli*?' Miss Lovell is gratified, though she thought some credit should go to the boy Robert.

Ramsay disagreed. True scientific credit should go not to the first observer but to the first person who thought the observation significant enough to report it. 'Mere observation, without record, is not enough.' If the observation is proved false? Then the record will be an error, with Miss Lovell's name attached as proof of folly.

The night drifted on and talk died down. The hurricane lamps were running low and at last there was talk of heading for home. The residents of Sandy Cape make their way up the sandhill and Ramsay and McIntosh start to pack up the folding telescope. Their last chance before they leave and nothing has happened.

There are stirrings in the deep. There often are. It's like creaking floorboards in an empty house. The deep is full of activity, and the forces of life and death do not cease when the sun goes down. Miss Lovell pauses on the track at the top of the headland and looks back at the men below. She calls out, for what is that down there? A shape, a large shape down by the edge of the water, a snake-like shadow of a long creature, rearing out of the water?

Miss Lovell cries, and her companions run to see what is happening. They strain into the darkness. They see shadows and shapes and stirrings, but each will report something different to the others when it is over.

Down on the beach, Ramsay runs to look. He trips over and the lamp goes out. He has sand in his eyes and he cannot see. He cries out for help and McIntosh stumbles through the darkness. Then McIntosh, too, cries out, for he has been thumped on the back and sent sprawling on top of his friend.

There is total confusion on the beach. Lighthouse keepers, children, Miss Lovell and the two men of science, and perhaps a Moha Moha, all run around in noise and the excitement of the moment.

McIntosh argues that he has been thumped by an illusion. He considers he has established that perceptual contagion is catching.

The years go by, and the Moha Moha isn't seen, at least by Miss Lovell. She lives in hope and daily she walks along the shore. It was probably only a long-necked chelonian after all, she thinks, but for a while it promised great things, and if it promised more than it provided in the end, she was not particularly unhappy.

Too much belief? Or not enough? It depends, on whether you've been the one to report the sea-serpent, or whether you're the one who only reads about it.

Power Play

In a pub on the coast men talk of the deep and the monsters that still may lurk there. Some say they have seen the Moha Moha, the sea-serpent of local legend. Others claim a mate who was there, or a friend of a friend who disappeared under mysterious circumstances, the sea flat, the day calm, yet the boat never returned, the men lost in the deep, for ever.

The sea-serpent of Sandy Cape is half turtle, half crocodile, with silvery scales, a forked tail and the speed of an eel. Real or imaginary, it is a creature of great beauty, one way or the other.

Max knows more than to seek truth from men in pubs. Ellie wonders about the deep and the monsters that may lurk there. That was in the early years of their marriage, when Max worked as an engineer on the sand-mining leases across the bay.

Ellie and Max drift and dream in the sun and the sand. They were the good times and she never knew it until later, much later. Though they did not really believe that things were so good they would very soon start getting worse.

Sand-mining dredges work their ways along the canals. Wild horses startle and run. The bush topples into the black sand; frail tree-roots are exposed to the air. Dredge and lift, tilt and thrust, the dredges take the dark sands of the earth and give them to the aerospace industry. Only a thin layer of crust is disturbed, only a thousand species killed, only a temporary death for the earth, which will one day rebalance things on the side of the bare and flat expanse rather than on the side of richness and diversity.

Here on the island built of sand there is an old lazaret, now in ruins.

Small wooden huts, collapsed to earth. The disease has run its course.

Ellie need have no cause for worry, as she gives birth to Oliver and brings him to the island. Leprosy no longer lurks. She has science to protect her baby from diphtheria, smallpox and the bubonic plague.

Max is restless and they leave the island. He moves into a new job in computers and does well. He takes his family south, inland to the plateau, where the sky is blue and the trees are grey. Silvery and dead, dark against the blue sky stand the grey trees. Where can sheep stand, when it is hot, where shelter, when it rains? Some say the sheep are the problem. Deliver the land back to its natural state and the troubles will pass. The dieback will stop, and the trees will recover and live again. They hope the illness is man-made. Otherwise it must be an Act of God, which leaves little room for hope.

Ellie sees trees that stand stark to the sky, dead. Oliver learns to talk. 'Tree,' he says and points to bare branches, a grey tree trunk. Tree. It is not a tree as Ellie remembers the trees of the islands, the trees of her youth. 'Tree!' says Oliver and Ellie must say 'Good boy!' as Oliver is born into language.

Trees have never been so grey before, never all at once. The reasons are complex and puzzling, and Max works on it for a while, till they find, in the end, no answer. The money runs out, and he must move on.

Down from the plateau and inland to where the silver dishes of the radiotelescopes listen to the stars. What do they hear? asks Oliver, older and wiser, and up to difficult questions. Ellie answers as best she can, but Max does better. He tells of worlds long destroyed, of a universe no longer wheeling serenely on its predestined course. Max tells a tale of chaos and rampage in the galaxy, of a primeval fireball, of black holes, variable quasars and neutron stars.

It's a wise child that knows a black hole and who asks where safety lies. Oliver wakes screaming at night and Ellie must soothe him (for Max is often absent, keeping the night watch on the computer). 'It's only a story,' she says. 'It's only Daddy's work.'

The dark shapes in the desert are tuned to the sky, eavesdroppers on the invisible pulsing at the heart of creation. The forces of the universe converge to a compact array of six radiotelescopes and a top secret low frequency nuclear submarine guidance facility. Little green men in outer space have not yet chosen to find us, but we will be ready for them when they come.

Oliver must go to school and on they move, south to the coast, to the big city and the world of private industry. To Max a company car and to Ellie a round of lunches, of waiting and being waited upon.

Now Oliver goes to school, Ellie has time to look to the world around her and she finds strange things are happening. The pylons of the power lines begin to bother her. She suspects they may hold hidden secrets. The monsters have marched out of the deep and are reaching across the plains to the city. But no one will notice, until it is too late.

I pass it every day, but I didn't notice the power line until the day they showed the television programme on radiation and health. Then I saw the pylons strung out along the freeway, across the floodplains at the bottom of the school oval, through the brickyard to the place where the freeway meets the level crossing. The power lines continue along the valley, and I turn up the hill towards home.

Current rushes along the power lines, electrons chasing tail to tail. Or so I thought. Now they say that strange things happen, that the surge is in the space outside the wires. They don't know for sure. Toasters work and garage doors open automatically. The city continues to exist, after a fashion.

They also say the radiation brings suicides and cancer. It sounds impossible but it may be true.

They tell her the correlation is unproven. Nobody knows if low frequency radiation gets out and gets you, deep in the cells of the body, a new danger and peril in the night. 'Cheer up,' they say. 'It may never happen.'

How do they know for certain? The spectrum never went that far, in the books they used at school. Twenty years on, and cells dance to a new rhythm. Broken genes and crumbling chromosomes, new powers, new forces turning the body electric, leading to difference, or death, or maybe even the Omega point of peace and cosmic unity. Who knows, with any degree of certainty? Ellie joins an action group and writes indignant letters to newspapers and to politicians.

Then Max moves on again.

Where is Max? Why doesn't he ring? I know he's gone, but I hoped he'd let us know what he's doing, how he's finding the new job. I thought he would keep in touch, at least for news of Oliver and his school and the small details of his life.

Ellie can't stop thinking thoughts which go round and round and spill out into a conversation with the washing machine or the aspidistra.

It happened so quickly. Max hated the job, and he applied for another. 'So simple, so common, so everyday an occurrence. Why should it be the end?' The aspidistra does not reply.

'It's the new boss,' Max explained, back in the days he lived with her, 'the one who wants us to hustle the contract research.' Max knows now he is a pure researcher. He must follow where the question leads and it may not always lead to money, at least at first. 'I thought I could play their game on my own terms,' he says, as he searches the papers for new jobs elsewhere.

Max says, 'I was wrong. It was a mistake, coming here. I can't take it any more. I want out.'

So I agreed with him and let him go! How was I to know that the new job meant Sacramento, that he would follow his work and leave us behind? That work was everything and we were nothing? I thought it was still the good times. It was good, I think. Though it is hard to remember, when it is over.

We were supposed to follow. But he wrote and said, 'Don't come.' So we stayed.

Oliver must now go home after school to an empty house and he likes it that way. He lets himself in and sits at the computer to play a game in which the forces of good battle the forces of evil in the underground kingdom of Azroth. Ellie sometimes feels she is an intruder into his after-school solitude. For the moment before Oliver smiles and says, 'Hullo!' Then she hugs him. Briefly.

Oliver is having some problems with school, with matrices and his algebra. 'Don't blame the single mum,' says Ellie to the cat. 'All the world's a single mum, and what about the absent father?' she asks the washing on the clothesline, and she's right. It was never part of the deal. She never promised Oliver she'd master the higher arithmetic for him, when she gave birth.

Though she learns to use the computer. She enters the realm of words which flow on to the screen and out into her eyes, into her head. The gap between is alive with waves of force zapping, zapping, zapping.

Pow!

The game of Azroth seems beyond her. She doesn't understand the rules.

'It's easy,' says Oliver. 'There aren't any rules.'

'That's what makes it difficult,' she replies.

Oliver explains carefully. 'You can travel anywhere you want. North, south, east or west.' Ellie travels north and finds an ogre in the attic. She goes south and there is an impassable chasm. She gives up, too easily.

'What is Azroth?' she asks Oliver.

'I don't know,' he replies. 'I've never found out what Azroth is.'

They make their dinner together. Oliver likes chips with everything and Ellie lets him have them, if he'll cook them. 'Okay,' says Oliver, who dwells with Azroth in her house.

Max, I have a vision of a link-up from the computer in my house to the computer in your office. My message will go bouncing up to a satellite and round the world and down to earth to hit your screen in Sacramento.

You can't hide. My message will seek you out. Search and destroy. Seek and kill.

If I can't do it, Oliver can. One day Security will be shot by a child hacker searching for his father. 'Hi, Dad, hi!' will flash up on the screens of the War Machine, pinning down the absent father, making him sorry he walked out. Scaring the shit out of him.

'Get out before they catch you,' Max will hiss at his end of the computer, typing furiously. He will say that to Oliver, his only son! But once Oliver gets in, he'll not let his Dad go so easily again and nor would I. I'd roam around for a while, seeing what else Max has up his sleeve, or in his computer memory.

I'd start the end of the world, from a whimper. I'd unleash some intercontinental ballistic missiles, if the mood took me. If I can crack the code.

Smash him with words. Smash him with the flashes of light that glitter before my eyes.

In the game of Azroth there is a trapdoor under the Persian carpet. That's the way to go. 'You can't go upstairs,' Oliver explains, 'because there's an ogre in the attic. The ogre can't get you if you have a lamp, but it's still the wrong way. Go back down the stairs and through the trapdoor and into the cavern under the ground.' Down the player must go, across the chasm into the underground kingdom.

North, south, east, west, stick to the path, follow the light, and maybe you'll find Azroth.

'Welcome to the Underground Kingdom.' But Ellie knows better. The Underground Kingdom is not everything it seems. It will be a trick. 'You are invited to a dinner.'

Ellie was invited to a dinner once, with Max, the rat.

'When you are under the ground,' says Oliver, 'you can see the air-holes up above, so high you can't touch them, and they're barred.' Some light enters, just enough to make you know what you've lost, and what you seek.

What is the meaning of the game? There may not be an answer to that question. 'You have to find the meaning of your adventure,' says Oliver. 'I haven't found it yet. You have to find a letter, one letter which will tell you. I don't know anyone who's ever found it.'

'Then how do you know it's there?'

Oliver rolls his eyes to his fringe and mutters, 'Unreal!'

Ellie retires to her thoughts.

I've lost Max and seek as I must, he's gone for good. I used to chatter over dinner and I suppose now that he must have found it – unnecessary. He would listen, I know that. He wouldn't say much, but every now and then there'd be a considered reply, a calm response which showed attention to my words. It's not enough just to have Oliver. Oliver will either give me his full attention, or none at all.

Max lived for his work alone, and I never knew.

At Sacramento he has it made. He works for the War Machine, that's true, but he can pose his own questions (within limits) and follow where they lead. It's the way of his world.

We were a moment's diversion along the path of his career.

Oliver goes to bed and Ellie takes her turn at the computer. She's on her way to Sacramento. She doesn't sleep very much any more. The words will come, the citadel will be breached, she will find Max.

He won't come willingly. She'll have to capture him. She'll take him to the kingdom of Azroth and imprison him. She will let him loose in the kitchen of the castle, where there is always plenty of food. Though he must learn to avoid the dwarf with the bloody axe.

Azroth is not without mercy. He will allow a stranger to stay, though he must play the game. Max will pay a certain price. It's only fair.

Particles flow from the screen. Forces surge through my body, twisting my mind, turning it to dark thoughts. The darkness is in me. The space between me and Max is half the world, but around the world the lines of force converge to link us. We spin in a web we cannot feel, threading a maze of lines we never see. Death, love, the love of death, forces and fields and flooded cells are all the gifts of power. Waves spill over the short end of the spectrum into Terra incognita. *New territory, uncharted waters, the place where 'Here be dragons', here Azroth dwells.*

It's easy, once you know how. To stage a computer capture. To hijack a man from Sacramento to the dungeons of Azroth. Of course they notice at the War Machine, when Max goes missing. Men in dark suits, with plastic smiles and hair cut short at the sides come to Ellie, seeking her out, asking her questions she could answer, but chooses not to.

After all, she cannot say, 'I have him safe in the computer kingdom of Azroth.' They would take her and put her away, and then who would help Oliver with his homework and his cooking? So Ellie tells the visitors about the pylons of the power lines, and the forces which surge between the wires and out into space, turning the body electric and the brain to jelly, until they see why Max may well have left for ever. She plays it cool by day, but at night she enters the Underground Kingdom.

Max, watch out! Snakes have titanium fangs! The sand-mining dredges will lurch on to land and pursue you. Look where the lazaret grows again from the dust and the dead return to their pain!

Flee the dread disease! Take the path which leads from the swamp. Go north.

Beware the sea, where the sea-serpent dwells. There is no refuge there. See where the Moha Moha rises from the waves, its skin glossy and smooth as an egg, its horns sharp as silvery spikes. It rears from the water, and look, a tough turtle carapace ridged with dinosaur plates. And its teeth! The teeth of the sea-serpent are waiting for you, if you seek to escape the terrors of the land.

Trust no one, especially the dwarf. He has a smile of welcome, but behind his back he holds a bloody axe.

Run from the darkness of evil and the power of the dead. Run through the silvery trees, the trees of the plateau, dead, all dead with the terrible sickness. Azroth prefers them that way, stark to the sky, without leaves, without life. Across the void the dieback comes, enters into the soul and causes the night terrors. Azroth has not signed the Geneva Convention. He plays dirty.

Run to the dish of the radiotelescopes; ride out on the wings of the messages which bound back into space. Look out for black holes and their marauding angels. Better to stay and be blown to cosmic dust in the next cycle of cosmic expansion, than be sucked down into the dark hole, into the bottomless pit. Soon you will know whose finger is on the trigger, whose mind directs the suction pumps of space, and whether it will choose benevolence or disengagement when the end is near.

The game will come to an end. Let him go. Release him from the spell! Don't leave him there, for ever!

Look how bewildered he is, look how his legs falter as he crosses the chasm, how his eyes tighten as he climbs to the light!

Max, stretch out and take my hand! I have the strength to let you go. You are free.

Is it my fault? The ether is wide. I cannot get over. Was it my fault? Tell me, 'No!' It was the pull of the other that led you from me.

Neither have I the wings to fly.

Look where the stalk of the mushroom cloud rises to the skies. Climb the stalk, that's the way to go, up into the sky.

'It's cold, it's cold, the ether is cold! Ellie, where are you?'

'Look down, Max, and see! See Oliver at home, see me at work! Look at us, please! Please.'

'It's cold, it's cold here. But I can see the earth turning beneath me, I can see the lines of force looping through the poles. I can travel out into space to ride the solar wind!'

'It's your choice, Max.'

'The Aurora is cold, but it lights the sky.'

'It's always been your choice.'

'Ellie, there's so much, so much to do, and I can do it!'

Max, you are free. Fly to the ends of your knowledge, though your knowledge may end us all.

The Invisible Woman

I bring my harp to the party, but nobody asks me to play.
My problem is that I am invisible. Let your light shine, says the text on the notice board outside the Church. Let your light shine and God will direct the beams.

My light is shining, but no one is noticing.

It's a common experience, I know. I'm not going to whimper about it, or complain. At least, that's what I say, gritting my teeth and snarling at whoever crosses my path.

Something must be done. Other people are being noticed. Their light shines and their beams show them off to advantage.

I am a woman, and my light makes me transparent. There's nothing else for it. I shall have to create my own glory for myself.

Day one on the path for Glory. I don't want to overdo it, not at first. I try it on Reginald, my boss. I stand so I reflect his glory. Reggie notices! He stands still for a moment, puzzled, appreciative. 'Why, you're gorgeous!' he says with enthusiasm, to me, his own reflection.

'I know,' I reply.

Reggie shakes himself, puzzled. He bangs his hand against his head, carefully, but with determination. He cannot believe what he has just said! He looks at me, sharply. I switch my glory off, and he sees me, good old Stella. He's safe again. He thinks his words have stayed in his own mind. He knows he's gorgeous. He looks through me at the typing pool beyond, and he crosses to chat up a dolly bird. I am not dismayed. This is victory! This is what I need! The first breakthrough into the new world, the first sign of the new me! Hurrah! I go home very pleased with myself.

Nigel at home, now he'll be the real test. Nigel specialises in not noticing. He's not around when I get home and it's the dog who greets me. I can't complain about the dog. Jessie has never treated me as the invisible woman. She appreciates my sterling qualities and always has. Still, I can try a spot of glory on the dog, just testing to see if the trick can work across the species barrier. I switch on and Jessie goes into a tizz! She sees me as the fridge! She's so excited, to see herself so far into forbidden territory, with her paw on the dog food! I pull out a few more stops. Jessie, look at me! I absorb the light from the refrigerator bulb, and I glow a faint mouldy green. Jessie backs off and sits down with a bump. I have become a green glow, but a green glow with a comforting Stella-like smell. Jessie is interested, but not confused.

I switch off. Jessie bounds forward to be fed.

I think I know what is happening. For so long I have been the pane of glass through which the light of others has shone. I used to see my position as a problem. Now I am discovering its hidden advantages.

I am a pane of glass. I have techniques for making myself opaque. Or I can reflect, like a mirror. With invisibility comes power. It's up to me to experiment further. Indeed, it's my duty. With such privilege, so much responsibility!

I quite like Nigel. It's not that we fight, or pummel each other. It's not as if a separation will achieve anything. I shall be as invisible to him as before, and he will continue not to notice I am no longer there. I live with Nigel and his habit of leaving his shoes under every chair and his tendency to grunt and scratch the side of his nose before delivering pronouncements on the personal and political ineptitude of the Prime Minister. I listen to Nigel on politics. All I am asking is that Nigel return the favour. I want him to hear my theory that I am a pane of glass.

Lack of communication, that's what they say is the problem with modern relationships.

Still, I try again. 'Nigel?' I ask. Nigel is busy painting the kitchen. He paints hi-gloss paint down strips of beading, which he will carefully nail down round the bottom of the skirting board. I shall have a kitchen which gleams, and Nigel will think it strange that I leap up and down and say, 'Notice me! Notice me!' while he is admiring the shine on the paintwork. It's all a question of priorities, he'll reply.

'Nigel, I think we have a problem,' I say. I am kind, but firm.

'D'you have a problem, Stella?' asks Nigel. 'I don't have a problem.'

I look at his brown hands and the veins which are starting to show through, throbbing faintly, on his wrists. 'Look at me,' I ask.

'What for?' asks Nigel.

I'll show him what for! I shimmer, I shatter, I explode into fragments at his feet. Nigel turns and crunches his way through broken glass. 'Stella, where are you? There's broken glass all over the floor! It's dangerous! I could have given myself a nasty cut! Why do you do things like this to me? Why do you always leave the kitchen floor in such a revolting state? I try, God knows how I try, I'm trying my best to do something with this place. I'm doing my bit. I'm up to my eyebrows in enamel and turpentine. Stella! Where are you?'

'In shards at your feet,' I reply, but all Nigel hears is the crunch of his boots on glass.

I retire to lick my wounds. I shall have to give it another go. I need to develop a strategic plan.

Life is a journey and my light must illumine the path. I give Nigel another try. 'There's something I must talk to you about.'

Nigel also has something he wants to talk to me about. 'Have you seen my multi-grip? I need it and it's not here. I try to keep my things in order, I try to have a place for everything, I try, I really do . . . '

I am firm, but brutal. 'Stuff the multi-grip! Watch this!' I fluoresce like a neon sign and I pour myself into some words. 'Try the cupboard under the sink,' I now read.

'What the hell's it doing there?' grumbles Nigel, as he tries the cupboard under the sink. 'If you want to borrow my things, that's fine, I'm not complaining, but why don't you ever put them back where they belong?'

It's not easy, being a pioneer. I am beginning to wonder about Nigel. Perhaps he is very thick indeed.

At work things are a little better. Reggie is thrown by the mirror trick when I do it again. For a moment he looks at me, he really looks at me, and he grows white around the eyes. I don't want to overdo it, so I quickly extend his own arm from my mirror in his direction. I grip his hand in his. He starts to shake. This isn't what I want at all! I don't want to be a terrorist! I switch and Reggie looks through me for something that is no longer here. He's starting to wonder about his sanity. He's not wondering about me, though.

I want to be noticed! And it's not working!

I am a pane of glass. I see I shall have to become an assertive pane of glass. I do not want to be a nasty pane of glass. No, my intentions are more or less strictly honourable. I want to be a warm and nurturant and loving pane of glass. I want recognition for what I am. Assertive, but not aggressive.

I begin to see what might be the problem. Up till now I have confined my activities to one person at a time. I have tried to change people individually. I might have predicted the outcome, that my contacts should think themselves drunk or deluded. Nigel can't even see the evidence before his eyes. Perhaps it's time he got himself some glasses.

What if I change my tactics and go for a mass conversion? What if I create an illusion that will be seen by a crowd? I shall try to change people collectively, rather than individually. It might be quicker, in the long run, to let my light shine for the multitude.

I take Jessie for a walk in the park after dinner. I have to have room to move, to think my problem through. It's dark, the clouds are low and I walk along the bicycle path to the oval.

As I walk, I brood, and as I brood I turn into a concave lens. I stop, and bring my beams to a focus. I focus on a bush and I become a burning mirror. The bush lights up and burns, and rolls along the path. I chase it and am consumed in the glory. A burning bush! I shall preach to the multitudes! But where are they, in the park at eight o'clock at night? I roll along, looking for them. Jessie follows. A burning bush, a dog and the beginning of a new world. Jessie's not worried. She follows behind. She has more faith in her nose than others have in their eyes.

There's a flasher lurking behind a tree, ready to show his all. In his eyes late walkers in the park are asking for it. He sees my transition and screams. 'Armageddon!' he cries, as he heads for the safety of the Gents'. I shout over the top of the wall: 'Vengeance is the Lord's!' but I do not bother to pursue him. I am no longer interested in individual conversion. I want to change the masses. I head for where the boys are doing football training. The lights are on around the grounds, so my glory dims a little as I roll, and it is a while before they see me. I mooch along, planning my strategy.

A voice must speak from the burning bush and what can I say to footballers? If I shout, 'Leave your game and follow me!' where, precisely, can I take them? Back home to Nigel? He'll point out that there's not enough beer in the fridge, and he'll be right.

Still, if I can change a football team, if I can get them to chuck over their coach and follow me, then perhaps I can change the world.

Our hopes are but dreams.

The football team catches me off guard. It's my own fault. I wasn't looking. The footballers have ceased their training and they're running alongside me, curious. I am surrounded. Worse! They seem to be worried about my impact on the park environment!

'Jesus, Dave, look! It's a burning bush!'

'It'll burn the clubhouse down!'

I am surrounded by men! Who have built-in fire extinguishers! Which they proceed to use! First one urinates and then another. Hiss and splutter! I am quite put out! It becomes a game to see who can go on the longest, throw the furthest. And on the run, as well! I'm a challenge for them.

'Hey, Jock, lend us a hand!'

'Have a go, Wade!'

'Good one, Farrelly!'

'Howzat?'

I've read in books about male rituals. But to find myself the object! I sizzle, I splutter and I fade.

'Slam it through the centre!'

'Sprint for the goal!'

'How's this for a long low pass?'

'Lay it on the line!'

And so on. Any more of this and I'm leaving. There was more of it. I left. I gathered my beams together and vanished into the infra-red range of the spectrum. I had to stay there a while to dry off. The humiliation! The stench! Jessie was confused and took off for home by herself.

So much for the burning bush. It worked with Moses, but then he was a man.

There's nothing wrong with the idea of mass conversion, *in principle*. It's just that I haven't got it working for me yet.

I consult a liberation group about tactics. 'The personal is political,' they tell me, and I must go back to where I started, with my relationship to Nigel. If individual revelation doesn't work, though . . . I watch my man, and I brood.

Back to square one, life in the suburbs. When Nigel turns to me in the early morning, before he must rise and go about the work of the day, I take him in my arms. 'Nigel,' I murmur into his ear, 'haven't you noticed something rather different about me this morning?'

'No,' says Nigel, breathing heavily and running his hands down my body.

Here I am, shimmering away, and Nigel doesn't even notice! He is making love to himself! I wonder if Nigel is gay.

'Nigel?'

'Wah?' says Nigel, his passion spent.

'Perhaps you really do need glasses.'

Nigel looks at me, then, but he thinks he is dreaming. His eyes shut, and he drifts back to sleep.

I can be a pane of glass, I can be a mirror, I can be a lens. I can distort the world, enlarge it, or shrink it to a bubble. I can reflect the stars, or creep into the world of the very small.

So much talent, without recognition. So much longing, without consummation. Absentmindedly, I stand at the kitchen door and I shrink the room until it becomes a world in a bubble of glass. Nigel's hi-gloss paint shrivels and cracks. I watch the dishwasher whizz through its cycle and the blender whirr cabbage into coleslaw fit for elves, and I start to question some of my assumptions. I have been wrong. I believed that the pane of glass would allow me to see the world, clearly, and without distortion. I believed that when I showed others their own reflection, they saw themselves as they really are.

I let the kitchen return to its proper size. Slowly it unfolds and grows, but look! What is happening? The fridge door is closing and there's a miniature Nigel behind it! He looks at me, the giant at the door, as I slowly shrink to meet him. He notices!

All Nigel says is 'Jesus, Stella!' Then he notices his new paintwork is cracked beyond repair.

It's time for me to go. This is the end of our relationship. I can see that now.

I walk the dog each day, and I try to work out what went wrong. I think we must have faltered where most couples come to grief. There is a natural tendency towards a natural end. It's what I've noticed with some of my friends. One partner is content to remain subdued in the murk of his old ways, while the other just keeps on glowing.

Where Are They?

1

Scratch the world of appearance and out leaps the hidden reality. All is revealed once the right question is asked. I know it now, but I had to learn it the hard way. Once there was me, and the rest of the world, and I never paid much attention to the rest of the world. Until I met Helena and we went to the Amazon to find the electric fish.

I never used to make the cosmic connections. I blame my friends for that. I was moving in the bedsitter crowd, spending nights on the floors of other people's rooms, making myself useful by doing budget cooking on their gas-rings. I have the basic skills of survival in London. As for the cosmic connections, I'm not talking astrology, the way my landlord friends do as they set about my food and get down to telling me what's wrong with me and my way of life. 'Typical, Leon, just typical. A true Cancer,' they'd say. 'Too perfectionist to ever start making the mistake of finishing anything' (this while stirring soy sauce into my stir-fry) or 'I bet you're a Virgo, laid back and lazy' (this while scoffing down my ratatouille, which takes a straight hour of chopping vegetables into delectably minute pieces). It never seemed to matter to them that they were always wrong about my star sign. 'I was born in January,' I can protest until I am purple, but it makes no difference. If people are intent on pointing out to you the flaws in your character and the error of your ways, if they feel it is their entitlement because it is their floor you are sleeping on, then that is their privilege. If you play their game in return and say, 'Typical

Gemini, always criticising,' they get uptight, and that's a new floor to have to trek out and find.

They know the answers. I never knew the answers. That's always been my problem. I was always looking. I know more now. I know the answer to one of the great questions that people have been asking ever since they looked up at the stars and could think in words, not grunts. Is there a hidden world behind the real world? Is there a world of light behind this dim glimmer of existence?

I met Helena, and I went to the Amazon. She was on the look out for a Canadian guy, she said, when she knocked on my door.

'You mean Perry?' I asked.

'Any Canadian guy,' she replied. She wanted someone to travel with, someone to keep the Latin American machismo at bay so she could go about her work.

'Will an Australian guy do instead?'

'Do you want to go to the Amazon?'

'Yes,' I said, at once. London was cold and wet. The Amazon sounded fine to me.

Of course it didn't happen quite that fast, but I persisted. It was my cooking that got her in the end, my ability to conjure up a meal out of a piece of old cheese, a tomato and some leftover pasta.

Helena told me about her work. 'I'm in electric fish,' she said. She had worked in fish for quite some time.

'Why?' I asked her.

'People drive you nuts,' Helena replied.

'I know the feeling.'

'Too many meetings,' she explained, 'too much fuss about ethics and everything. Take all these tape recordings I make with fish. If I did it with people it would take ten times as long! First I'd have to get their consent and the permission of the top brass, then I'd have to work out what they really mean when they talk to each other, apart from what they say they mean. And then they'd only disagree with me! They'd argue with my findings! They'd say that wasn't what they meant at all! That I had it all wrong! They'd argue back! It's all too much! So I went into fish, instead.'

Because fish don't argue back. Nor do they provide a long list of one's personal failings. I warmed to Helena's fish. I said I could get to like working with them.

2

Where are they, the voices from the void? Helena takes up her notebook and tries to get her thoughts in order for the coming interview with Jerry and the top brass. It will be important. She will have to convince them that her fish are special fish, electric fish, weakly electric fish, not strongly electric fish like electric eels which can stun and sometimes kill their prey with a bolt of electricity from their tails. The green knife fish and the banded knife fish do it differently. They fizz with a gentle current all their lives. Bees buzz and cicadas drone, and electric fish pulsate. That will be part of her story.

She will ask them to imagine a flashlight battery at one end of a river three miles long. The fish can pick up that signal! Why? How? That's what she needs to know, and that's what she must convince them. She must go to the Amazon to find out. She will tell them that there may be some cosmic connections to be made. They say a message from a CB radio may be picked up far out in space. Why not a message from a fish? Fish may be more than just fish. They may be heralds of a new age.

She will tell them what she knows already, that the fish use their electric sense to communicate with each other. She will point to the fact that she can tape their conversations without troubling with the ethics of the situation.

She has to work out a strategic plan for funds. She has to put herself in the place of Jerry and the top brass at The Search, and think like they do, to work out what they'll go for.

'Telepathy' she writes in her application. Why not? The wilder the idea, the more they'll sit up and take notice! They won't care about electric fish, as such. She must use her ingenuity to get their money. Trips to the Amazon cost the earth! And she will need an assistant, someone like Leon to help with the equipment and the heavy work. They will appreciate that. A woman alone will need male protection. Who knows what may happen otherwise? The lady Amazons of ancient times had no problem, but Helena is not built like them. She is small and intense, and hopeless with a bow and arrow.

Telepathy – how to angle the idea? An electric sense might be a step on the path to silent communication! It seems to work that way for the fish. They know the tides, and most likely the orientation of the earth in space, they know about each other and other fish, where they are, how many and whether they belong to the same or a different species. They know the sex of the others and their sexual ripeness. In short, they use electricity to chat each other up, and to know what's what and who's where. Smart fish.

Helena should get the help she needs now she has placed her work in a broader context. Even if she does not yet believe what she is saying.

She will get the funds.

3

When Helena said I could come with her, my heart took a leap. I'd bummed around for some years since dropping out of uni in Australia – India, Turkey, anywhere where living was cheap. Something I read somewhere said it all – to travel out is to travel within. The force is in you, that's the modern message. Surely the Amazon would provide some kind of insight! The Amazon! The wildest, biggest river of them all! But there was so much I didn't know, before I went. I knew about mosquitoes and malaria, and I took my chloroquine. I knew the river was wide and fast, large and long, and that the jungle it drained was doomed one day to die. I knew about heat and slime and fungus and the danger of death. But I didn't know about the flooded forests, or the fish that swim through the trees and eat the flowers and fruit and seeds on the forest floor. So many ways of eating and of being eaten. So many ways that death may come, from all directions, above, below, the circle of water all around. The world of the waters is the world beneath us all.

I didn't know about the enchanted village, where people live under the water, drowned yet not doomed to death. They carry on their lives as best they can, as they did before the night the village slid down from the river bank and into the water. Cocks still crow and turkeys carry on with their continual burble, though the village floods with water to their sky. Sometimes people slip out from the village and walk along the river bank, but if they are seen, if someone calls them, they look up, away, then silently slide back into the water, and down, down again to tend the underwater country.

They do not like the fishing boats working up above them, or passing over their village. They do not want fish hooks and nets descending from their sky, or the constant putter-putter of boats above, and the locals respect their wishes.

'You never told me about the enchanted village,' I said to Helena.

'You never asked me,' she replied.

I walked and talked with people who knew the stories, and people who could tell me what they were saying. These were the stories of the enchanted village, the spirit world of the river and the largest sea-serpent of them all, the *cobra grande*.

'They're having you on, Leon. They're telling you the stories they use to scare the children,' Helena said.

I had to agree. 'The question is, why are they telling me tall stories? What function do the stories serve?' It was the same kind of question that bothered me in London, with my landlord Perry and his belief in the power of the stars.

We were eating fish that night, cooked local style on green twigs bent over the fire so that the fish was smoked rather than baked. We ate it with a sauce of chillies crushed in a little water.

'This is good, Leon!'

'Better than last time you came here?'

'Of course! I usually eat out of tins on these trips.'

'Tins are the pits.'

'So is logistics. You try to do all the planning, and the fund-raising, and the science, and the cooking as well! Something has to go!'

'It's because you're English,' I told her.

'Why?'

'Remember Captain Scott? Of the Antarctic?'

'Why?'

'It's what he ate. The most revolting food. Lumps of solid animal fat! Dry biscuits! No vegetables. No vitamins. That's why they never made it. Scurvy! The French explorers had more sense. They always took the best champagne and caviar. It's no more trouble, and it's nicer.'

'Oh, tins are no trouble at all,' said Helena. 'They're so quick and easy! All you have to do is rip off the lid and wolf down the contents.'

'Ugh!'

'One tin for first course, another tin for second course. In any order. Peaches first then steak and kidney. Cold. Out of the tin. No washing up.'

'You're having me on,' I said. 'That's just a story to scare the children.'

'I always use a fork.'

Sometimes I wonder about Helena, whether she only does it to tease me. Then again sometimes I think she is being perfectly serious.

Of course we were a curiosity to the people of the village. Here was a woman who was fishing, though for what? And a man who was cooking the catch. We never ate the subjects of our experiments, the banded knife fish and the green *Gymnotus carapo*, much preferring the paraya, which lives off fruit, and the orange-tailed *pirarara*. Plain cooking, but delicious.

The locals asked me as many questions as I asked them, and I told them tales of London, and life in a bedsitter, and my landlord Perry, and his claim that the stars were in control of my personality.

They nodded and agreed. 'Of course,' they said. It is my fate. Everyone sees the cosmic connections, everyone but me.

Until it happened.

4

Helena takes up her notebook and writes up her field notes by the light of a kerosene lantern. Insects thud against the glass as she broods about her work so far. She has come to the jungle because things go wrong with the fish when they are confined in the glass tanks of the laboratory. Echo-location, that seems to be the problem. The fish are put out of kilter by something in the artificial laboratory environment, perhaps by the regular shape of the aquarium, and their signals become increasingly wild until they die. She needs to record them more naturally, in their home territory.

She notes the results of their daily excursions. Each day they venture with Luco the fisherman into one of the local streams, up a way to the shelter of the shallows where the electric fish reside. She has tests for electroreception, and equipment which will measure the relation of their signals to the earth's bioelectrical and geophysical fields. She needs to know how the fish sort the conflicting demands of their electric sensory system. They can locate themselves in space, while sending messages of courtship and dominance and more general inquiries. They relate to the forces of the river, and the forces of the earth, and – who knows? – the forces of interstellar space.

She makes notes of what happens during the day and the night, when she beams in her own signals in the playback experiments. If she places a dipole model fish in the river, and if she chooses a 'threat' sequence of pulses, then the dominant fish will attack the model. If she indicates a readiness to mate, then the dominant male will go into a frenzy of unrequited passion.

She likes the power.

She will need to know more about the way the signals move out into space. How can they tell where she is, when she calls? She writes her notes into the night, while the village sleeps, and Leon dreams of wide lakes and thrashing monsters.

5

'Who'd be a fish?' says Helena, directing her electrical signals into the stream.

'I thought you'd like it, for a while,' replies Leon.

'Yes, and no,' she says. 'I'd like to find out more, but then I'd like to change back into myself again, so I could tell the world. And it's a tough world down there, it's eat or be eaten.'

The fish aren't fooled by the playback signals when they come from the land. If they call first and Helena answers, there is an extra hiccup in their output, an additional blip in their responses, just to show they know. It's different when they talk to each other and when they think they are alone. It shows they are curious fish, interested and keen to know more about the world. If some extra-terrestrial intelligence were to contact us, we'd answer, wouldn't we? or so Helena thinks. Or would we just keep quiet, and hope they'd pack up their signals and go away, disappointed? Just in case they came in conquest.

Helena is quizzed by the local dominant banded knife fish about whether she is available for mating. She beams down her answer in a series of broken pulses. She tests them out. They must wonder at a large electric fish that walks on land. They're not stupid. They can put two and two together. Nearly.

Most days are much the same. Each day Helena and Leon travel out to the field, with Luco as their guide through the wild waters into the quiet streams. They take note of the records made during the night, when the fish are at their most active electrically, and set up the equipment for the night to come. Each night they return to base camp at the village. Still it's never routine, doing the same thing day after day, not on the edge of the primeval forest, where birds shriek high in the trees, and animals forage noisily but unseen across the forest floor, and fish send their electric signals through the waters. They live with people skilled in the ways of the river, whose explanations for the horrors and highlights of their lives are as matter of fact as ours, and no less extraordinary. Who would believe it, a sea-serpent 200 metres long? Who would believe it, that a man should walk on the moon? Who would believe that there is an evil water spirit which steals the soul of anyone whose shadow passes over it? Who would believe that a malevolent spirit steals the souls of those who work on the bombs which may end us all?

Helena works with the capacity to put up with tedium while waiting for that moment of insight which comes, when it comes, all too rarely. What she wants are the words in print which will establish her credentials in her world. That is why she sits in the jungle, removing leeches from her bloodstained trousers and battling the ants and the mosquitoes. If at times Leon looks to the leafy canopy far above and wonders what they are doing scrabbling away at the surface of knowledge in such an arbitrary fashion, Helena has no doubts.

'Why bother?' asks Leon one day, when the rain pelts down and the leeches fall from the trees, and the equipment is too damp to use, and the steamy heat grows mould on the backpacks. 'Why do this kind of work? Why not go in for land snails in Bermuda, like the guy on television?' He'd looked relaxed and warm and comfortable, and rich and famous.

Helena smiles and shrugs off the land snails in Bermuda. She wants more.

Leon works with the will of someone who is looking for something, and feels he is on the verge of finding ancient secrets, future marvels.

6

Helena records the events of the evening in her notebook.

Out late, too late, setting up last crucial experiment. Left it running overnight. Should test how far the signals travel. The final test. Nearly the final test for us all. Engine failed in boat on long trip home. Nearly swept away down the river. Leon and Luco no help. Leon went into a tizz and Luco got offended at some imagined insult. Useless! Had to do everything myself. Glad field trip is nearly over. Leon going troppo?

7

Leon tells it differently.

We were kept busy that day of the final test. It took us longer than we thought to set up the last experiment. It was late when we turned back to the village. Dusk came suddenly, and sunset, soon over. Magical, though, for those brief moments that it lasts, while the wind ripples the water and the current flows strongly underneath, the blue deepens and the greys darken, and the sky is streaked with red. Birds call in the dusk, from hidden nests high in the canopy. Insects swoop like hawks. The musty smell of rotting vegetation falls from the tops of the flooded trees. New life feeds on old as the waters fall.

Suddenly the engine stopped, just like that. No warning, just silence, and we began to drift downstream. We drifted for a while, helpless, then we pulled up with a jerk, as if the brakes had been applied. The boat was at rest, while the current flowed underneath, and the wind tossed the tops of the trees, and the sky changed colour overhead to black. Everything was happening, yet nothing was happening. We were like the inhabitants of the enchanted village, who wake one morning and find themselves living under the water. They must continue with life as they have always known it, though they must now dodge the hooks which descend from the sky and the nets which dredge down to the streets.

We sat there, *encantados*, enchanted.

'*Cobra grande*?' I asked Luco but he merely shrugged his shoulders and rolled a cigarette. He was prepared to wait it out. He was fairly calm about it all, considering.

'They say that *cobra grande* can do this, stop the engine of a boat,' I told Helena.

'Now he tells me,' she said. She was trying to turn on a flashlight, without success. 'I wonder how *cobra grande* got so smart about Western technology.'

It was like being caught in a traffic jam, only there wasn't any traffic. Any visible traffic. Who knows what goes on in the spirit world? Perhaps there was one mighty spirit jam that evening on the river and we had to wait while other more important beings went on their way. The stories serve a function. They serve to let us know where we stand. Nowhere special, where the other world is concerned.

'Whatever happens, if *cobra grande* appears, you mustn't look into its eyes.'

'I won't,' Helena promised. 'It's so dark I can't see a thing.' She gestured at Luco to get moving on the engine. Luco shrugged his shoulders and looked helpless.

'It has bright blue eyes and they're three feet apart.' I tried to paddle the oars in the water, but it was like rowing through treacle. 'Don't look or you will become *assombrada*. You will run a fever and become delirious and die.'

Helena was sceptical. Someone must have looked, to know, and lived to tell the tale, she pointed out. She was rather terse.

To become *encantado* is rather like most other things in life. It is remarkable how quickly one becomes used to it, how it is hard to start imagining things could be otherwise. The impossible happens and everything is the same, yet nothing can ever be the same again.

Helena did not share my moment of truth, not then. 'Why are we sitting here?' she asked. She kept trying with the engine, but nothing happened.

Our guide meditated on his cigarette. 'Useless,' muttered Helena, but what else is there to do, when enchantment strikes? Shine a light in the darkness.

'Just when I was starting to get some results,' says Helena. 'Just as I was about to get the Nobel Prize.'

'No one ever gets the Nobel Prize for fish.'

'There's always a first time.'

The force released us as suddenly as it caught us. The boat started to take off down the river, just as Helena got the engine going again. We were silent for the rest of the trip into the village. We told people what had happened. *Encantados*, but no harm done, that was the general verdict. It happens. It's like getting flu and getting over it. Or dying in the attempt.

8

Fish, fish, electric fish, Helena writes in her notebook. The words march down the paper. Fish, fish, electric fish, come and talk, we know you're there. We come in peace, perhaps, and all we want to know is how you do it. What is it like, to have an electric sense? What is it like, to send out lines of force which pulse out into the water, into the air, into space, curving towards an unseen target? Forces and fields, tugs and pushes, pushes and pulls, dots and dashes, yes and no, off and on, and a conversation may pass through water and beyond into the far reaches of the universe. All it takes is sense and sensitivity, and who knows what lies out there, waiting to receive the call?

Extraterrestrial electric fish, that's my bet, says Helena.

Giant cobras, stirred from their muddy sleep, says Leon, scaring himself into hypnagogic visions of heaving serpents with tongues of flame.

There is a commotion in the night. The river is alive with action. Forces stir the deep. The water froths. No one sleeps. They keep guard, watching to see if the village will start the downwards slide into the water.

The last night, the last day, the day to end the task, comes at last at the close of the night of turmoil. Night ends, and the moment comes when the task is near its end, when they will sift what is relevant, discard what is adventitious and pack for the long journey home.

If the boat comes. But it does. Luco is accustomed to nights of commotion. It's all the same to him, life above and life below the water.

Luco is the noble savage, to Helena.

Luco is a man fully in tune with the forces of nature, to Leon. Though Leon cannot approve of cigarettes.

It's another day, another river to Luco, unnoble savage and lover of diesel engines.

At the experiment site everything was in chaos. The mud on the river bank was folded in on itself, like molten lava solidified in water into ripples and ridges. Paths were forced through the reeds, the grass. Mud and lily roots, reeds and hollows, electronic equipment and wires, nature and technology crumpled and mixed. Vandals at work. Natural vandals. Cosmic vandals. The universe of chaos and confusion.

'This wrecks it,' says Helena. 'This is the end.'

'Or is it?' says Leon. He finds the equipment all over the place, but functioning still.

Helena is cheered. She picks up the recording devices, the tracking devices. Sturdy army gear, good at thirty degrees below zero and sixty above, made to survive the impact of bullets and the splatter of blood. Big enough to give a fit of indigestion to any cobra crazy enough to eat it. That's what Leon thinks.

Whatever happened, it was still recording, though pointed at the skies.

Leon knows one answer. 'Check it out!' he says, excited. 'See if there are any new signals on it. See if *cobra grande* is an electric fish! Think what it would mean: the first scientific proof of a sea-serpent! It will be like finding the Loch Ness monster! We'll be rich and famous!'

'And the laughing stock of London, Paris, and New York!' Still Helena is prepared to listen. She went looking for something else, but chance favours the prepared mind and she knows it.

It took her time to work out. It wasn't easy. She had to analyse the signals and feed the information into the computer.

I knew Helena had found something. I knew it by the speed and anxiety with which she worked and the whiteness that grew about her eyes. I couldn't believe it, either. It's often the case. You go looking for one thing and you find another. It hasn't quite got me believing in astrology, though, but I have a lot more respect for sea-serpents, and for enchanted villages.

Helena went straight back to London, and I stayed on, as I'd planned. I wanted to see more of the strange places where the underworld of enchantment flows beneath the everyday. I went to Ecuador and lived for a while with the Indians of Otavalo, and then I pushed on to Peru.

9

They like her results, the people from The Search. She'd found it for them, the first signs of extraterrestrial life. She'd gone looking for something else, for evidence of telepathy, and she'd discovered something entirely different, though equally important.

Of course it is disappointing, to find that the aliens who were the first to contact earth should be interested in talking exclusively to electric fish. 'Where are you?' Yes, we knew that would be one question extraterrestrials would ask when they made contact, though whether we would choose to tell them the answer was quite another thing. That they should be interested exclusively in questions of location, size, sex, and sexual ripeness of just two species of freshwater fish is something of a surprise.

People imagine they would ask the big questions, 'Is there a God?' and 'Is there Eternal Life?' But the extraterrestrial intelligence didn't want to know about matters unrelated to food and reproduction, and that will be the gist of her report to Jerry and the top brass at The Search. It is the truth, and she can't be expected to deliver more than that.

She'd enjoyed having Leon along on the trip. He was like her fish, none too bright, but decorative and curious. He asked some of the right questions, even if he found the wrong answers. Travel broadened his mind into a bundle of elastic fibres capable of stretching to infinite limits. Sceptical of astrology in its London version, he'd swallowed the tall stories of fishermen without blinking.

The problem with Leon was that he had plenty of theories, but few facts to which to relate them. Though she would always be grateful to him for one thing. She no longer ate cold hunks of beef out of cans any more. She will take some French champagne along with her on her next trip.

Of course Leon was up against it, trying to find the answers. She never told him half the story. She didn't tell him she was working for The Search, or that the trip was much more than it seemed. In the search after truth, she had to tell serious lies.

She suspects that Jerry and the top brass will be disappointed. They had assumed that whoever is out there, if it is trying to contact us, will be smarter than we are. They say this because we are not really trying to find them, at least by beaming signals out into space. We are merely searching for their signals to us.

Leon asked the right question – what caused the problem on the river, the evening the engine failed for a few brief moments? What force dragged the equipment down a grass tunnel halfway into the jungle? He found the wrong answer. It wasn't a giant Brazilian water-snake. Forces were at work, but their source was extraterrestrial. They were not the forces of the spirit world.

What was still exciting about that last day on the river bank was that she'd found something she'd often wondered about, but never thought she'd discover – evidence from the stars! She worked out the position in the sky from which the signals came, though the signals came for them, and not for us. She'd taped one of the most important conversations of them all, the first intergalactic exchange of information between life forms! She'd worked out the gist of the first interplanetary message! It wasn't her fault that the content turned out to be trivial.

She will probably go back to working with people now. Telepathy still beckons. There's nothing more to discover, with fish.

9

Jerry drafts his report to the top brass.

Divide and conquer, always a good strategy. Don't let the left hand know what the right hand's doing. That's why they don't know the extent of our interests here at The Search. That's why we separate the workers from each other. If everyone knew what everyone else was doing, if there was a free and frank exchange of information, then they might get to see a little of the overall picture, and they'd get a shock! These people, they've got plenty of theories, but no brains! They know nothing! Absolutely nothing! They think we're just here to provide them with the money and the good life. Ha! I've got a thing or two I could tell them!

The whole story, that's my job. I sit at the centre, they report to me and I fit all the pieces into the puzzle.

The way I see it, it's Us versus Them. Always has been. Always will be. Fundamental law of life. In this case, it's the terrestrials against the Giant Walking Talking Electric Fish of somewhere near Alpha Centauri. They've come and found us. So they must have a good reason for their search. I know at present that all we have is a signal from a distant planet, but the next thing they'll do is they'll be arriving to take us over. They'll be on their way to turn us into fish-food.

More than at any other time of our planet's history we need those missiles in space. The more of them the better. Pointing outwards.

I'll get the money for the project. I always do.

The Children Don't Leave Home Any More

The children don't leave home any more. They stay on and expect to be loved, once they are well into the age of reason. They may make various attempts at escape, smiling and waving with joy the first time they take off, butterflies from the cocoon. Six months later back they come, bringing their live-in lovers and their dogs.

I wake in the morning and I find strange bodies on the floor of my house, people I have yet to meet over morning coffee. They lie curled up in sleeping bags or on the couch, back to the womb, my womb, though I cannot recollect I ever gave them birth. They are warm and comfortable, and sheltered, and my children's friends.

I have friends, too, and my friend Jean thinks it is ridiculous. She tells me I am a doormat, a convenience and a dill. She never had children of her own, she says, because she saw what a trial they were to other people.

'I rather like it,' I tell her.

'In my day, Marion,' she replied, 'if you wanted sex, you had to leave home for it, and that was that.'

'Ah, the good old days!'

'Next it'll be grandchildren, and you'll find yourself running a crèche.'

She may be right.

It came to me one day, the strangeness of the way we live now, when we went for a walk along the track at Miller's Landing. There we were, the children who don't leave home, my children and Paul's, Catherine and David. Paul was with us that weekend, though he's often away. The children don't leave home any more, but the father often does. Cause and effect, perhaps.

We were walking along a nature trail marked with numbered signposts and reading from a brochure explaining the wonders of nature. Together we marvelled at the banksia and its ability to regenerate after fire, and its purpose as the natural larder of the bush. Gold-dusted banksia flowers lay at our feet, with seedpods smashed open and savaged by rampaging cockatoos, while in the distance glinted the calm blue-grey seas of the bay.

There's something special about walking in the bush. It brings on philosophical reflections and thoughts move easily from the particular instance to its cosmic significance. Catherine said, 'I know what we can do! Why don't we have a nature trail around our kitchen?'

Everyone knew exactly what she meant. The ants in the kitchen tidy. The spider webs up in the corner of the ceiling. And worse! We have a cupboard through which we can run a nature trail!

'The moths. Those small white moths that fly out of the cupboard when it's opened!'

'I've seen them. They've picked a funny place to live.'

'I dunno. Pretty smart really. There's plenty of food.'

'They don't live there. They hatch there. Then they fly out of the cupboard and off to the next one.'

'They hatch there? Yuk! In stuff we eat?'

'And the spider! There's a spider in the corner of the cupboard, that eats them.'

'The complete cycle, from predator to prey!'

'Isn't nature wonderful?'

And so on. The point I want to make is this. Everyone had noticed what was happening. And no one had done anything about it! No one took the initiative and cleaned out the cupboard! And I have to include myself in this indictment. We each of us assumed it was someone else's job. We can all live together, and notice the nature trail, and yet do nothing, individually. It takes a collective bushwalk to bring it all out into the open.

Of course, Paul has a bad back and Catherine believes in the sanctity of all non-human forms of life. There are plenty of excuses for inaction. Really, though, it's a question of our times, a question of power in the family, a question of just who it is that other people expect to act on their behalf. A question of the children who don't leave home any more, because housing is expensive, and jobs are hard to get, and home is warm and comfortable and their own.

It is clear they expect me to notice things, to organise things, to tell them what to do next. It is clear that I expect them to be fully autonomous self-actuating human beings.

Who is being unreasonable?

I am, they will say to me. Not unreasonable, exactly, but carping, complaining unnecessarily, about unimportant things like cupboards, when we all know who is starving in Ethiopia; when there is a demonstration to attend, against the American installations at Pine Gap or the Save the Rainforest campaign; when time spared from job and house-hunting may be better spent reading a book or applying three shades of eye-liner in ever decreasing circles.

There must be another way to live, now the children don't leave home any more.

The search is on. 'I know! Rosters! Let's have rosters, the way we did when you were children, and you shared the jobs, like feeding the cat and drying the dishes.'

'Oh, a roster,' said Catherine, 'that won't be necessary. I'll be moving out, as soon as I can find a place to stay. I mean, I know I can move any day, to Palmerston Street. It's just that I need to find a place that'll take the cat. So don't bother with a roster. It'd be a waste of your time, drawing it up.'

David was all sweet reason. 'I'll grant you, we needed a roster, back then, before we got the dishwasher. Things were different, then.' To show how different everything can be now, he stands and clears the table and stacks the dishes and wipes down the kitchen benches and really, really, I can see that I have nothing at all in the world to complain of. They are kind and nice, my children. But they are not consistent. They will always agree happily with my suggestions, but they must wait till my words fall. They will always point out, calmly and agreeably, if my request is not something they can see their way free to granting, not here, not now, but of course, some other time when it will be personally more convenient to them.

They think it's best for them, now they are adult, to be free spirits, to help out, as they see fit, but not to be trammelled, not to be controlled, by too much management, too much organisation. 'It's only housework, Marion. You must rise above it. There are much more important things to do in life.'

I heard a scientist on the radio, scoffing at the way the research grants went that year. 'This bunch of sociologists!' he said. 'They get a grant for doing research on *housework*! While real science, physics and chemistry, is starved for funds. It's outrageous!' I bet he never does any housework. I feel it, in my bones.

I greet the latest arrivals on my floor one Sunday morning. I've met them before. I know who this lot are. In two weeks they'll be off to South America. Meanwhile there are landlord hassles, and do I mind?

'Why South America?'

'Europe's too expensive these days,' sighs Jenny.

Martin agrees. 'The exchange rate! It's ridiculous. The Australian dollar gets you nowhere, most places. South America is all we can afford.'

It's true, what I said to my friend Jean and what she can't understand. I rather like the drop-ins. My children and my children's friends fill the house with noise and confusion and uncertainty, and I enjoy it now Paul is away most of the time in Canberra. I have the house and the children in Melbourne, while Paul has Canberra and freedom. He chose to go and I chose not to follow. He couldn't bear the department down here, and got a transfer. But I didn't go then, for various reasons: the children, their schools and my work. All my contacts are here. I thought – I shall leave it a year, then I shall go. Paul comes home once a month and I go up to him, now and then, when I can. It's an arrangement which suits him and with which I have learned to live.

I shall leave it a year, then I shall go, I said once. But I still haven't gone. There's so much that must happen first. There's Mother, Paul's mother. It breaks you up. She comes from the home on Sundays if she's well enough, and she sits at the piano. She picks out the tune of 'Home Sweet Home'. She plays it again and again and we all listen and grow thoughtful. Home sweet home, the grey shining skies of the home of her childhood in Scotland, or the home of her marriage, in British Borneo before the war. Not the place where she now lives, though it is clean and moderately caring, for a nursing home. I rush around trying not to notice too much. 'The Virgin Mary,' she says, if

I ask what she is thinking about as she plays. 'Cats.' Home Sweet Home.

The children and their friends may eat separately. Vegetarian, usually, though they eat steak at other people's houses. Jenny helps me prepare the food and Martin stands in the middle of the kitchen and gets in the way. They're on their best house-guest behaviour. Towards the end of their stay they will become more forgetful. My house will become more like their home.

Mother walks carefully, with the air of continual rediscovery that one leg, placed after the other – and why only two legs? Are there any more to follow? – will propel the human body across the floor. Jenny says, 'I like the colours of your dress,' and Mother examines her sleeve as if colour is a brand new experience, and one she must take time to consider. Paul fusses her into a chair, and she enjoys the male concern and the small glass of beer.

My children Cathy and David laugh about the plans for South America, half-envious, though. They can't leave home, that way, until they land their jobs and their independence. David tells tales of giant leeches that lie in wait and drop from the jungle trees and the Pampas bug that bites and injects parasites into the blood of travellers. 'They wriggle into the heart and the gut, and settle there for ever,' says David, the friend of travellers.

'Don't listen to him. I expect Bogotá will be no worse than Paris, really,' says Catherine. 'Think of all the advice to travellers. It used to be about pickpockets. Now it's about bombs. I've heard they blow up your luggage if you leave it in the trains.' She offers her grandmother some celery and yoghurt. 'No thank you, Marion,' says Mother firmly.

'What about Egypt? Remember when Barry went, and said he felt perfectly safe all the time?'

'Yeah,' says Martin, 'people tell you terrible stories,.but I don't know what they know, or if they know what they're talking about. Like giant leeches that swing from the trees, and the bugs that leap from the Pampas.'

David grins.

'It's all those soldiers rattling round everywhere with machine guns,' says Catherine as she arranges her lunch, slices of raw vegetables, a pot of yoghurt, three bottles of vitamin tablets and a homeopathic remedy for something. Something expensive.

Mother is settled and the fork placed on her good side, where she can see it. She makes herself at home; she leans over and takes the food from other people's plates.

'Those machine guns. They must use them, sometimes, to kill people.'

'But the funny thing is, it makes you feel safe.' Catherine gives her grandmother some parsnips. 'Take Melbourne, now, it's not like Cairo. I'd be worried here, if I saw submachine guns out everywhere. But there, when you see them, you think, well, I won't be mugged just now . . . '

'Except by a man with a machine gun.'

'I'd rather meet a man with a machine gun than a man with a machete. Any day.'

'Do I get a choice?' someone asks.

'We had a man with a machete in casualty, just last week,' said Jenny. 'The cops brought him in. He was wandering round a park with a tomahawk in one hand and a rope in the other. They questioned him, but couldn't hold him. So they brought him in to us. There's no law against it, apparently. He didn't know what he was doing, why he was there with a tomahawk and a length of rope.'

'It's a free country. Does he have to have a reason?'

'That's what they said. But the rope had a hangman's noose at one end.'

'That's different.'

'He was just walking round with an axe and a hangman's noose, and there's nothing anyone can do about it.'

'That's what Bogotá will be like. Everyone will have a machete and a length of rope with a noose at one end.'

'So you'll feel quite at home,' says Catherine, retrieving her drink from Mother.

I need a man with a machete to organise the housework for me. I need someone who will cut a swathe through the peace of the house, and wake people to their obligations.

They say it's best to wait it out. They say, the psychologists on radio who are experts in such things, they say one day the children will emerge neat and tidy and well-organised, and will forget about this part of their lives. Or they will regard it as an inexplicable but idly amusing interruption, the kind of thing that happens with the hassles of unemployment and the searching, searching the papers for work. I've asked the radio man on the talk-back psychology show. I rang up and told him the problem, and he said, 'Don't be a doormat.'

'I am not a doormat.'

'What makes you think you're not a doormat?'

'It's not that they walk all over me. It's just that they don't see the work that needs to be done.'

'I can understand how you must be feeling.' Useless. 'Have patience. Wait it out.' It's been years, now. 'Don't do their work and see how things will change.' They don't. 'They will notice, they will change, they will start to appreciate the problem. They must work this thing through for themselves.' So must we all. 'Suck it and see.' I certainly will not. 'It's all your fault. Lack of parental guidance and discipline when they were young.' I bet his wife ties his shoelaces for him. 'I wish I knew what I could do to help.' That's what they all say. They learn it at psychology school.

Perhaps new forms of technology will show the way, or human nature will change to housework-oriented ends. So all around will be sunshine and light and co-operation, and people will dwell together and know how to do it properly.

And the housework will do itself! Dust will vanish from the floors. Each front door will have a dog entrance, complete with automatic dog vacuum cleaner, which will dust the dog down electronically before it enters the house, removing loose hair and fleas and worse.

Dinner plates will be intelligent machines which will scrape themselves into the rubbish and set off on tiny motorised wings into the dishwasher, through the cycle and out at the other end to stack themselves neatly in the cupboard.

Clothes will fall to the ground where they are discarded and in the middle of the night small anti-gravity devices will be activated in the labels, and the clothes will float silently into the air. The level of dirt in the fibres will be measured, and some of them will waft themselves into the washing machine, while others rearrange themselves into the cupboard in properly co-ordinated blocks of colour.

Shoes will shuffle silently in pairs across the floors, self-polishing as they arrange themselves in neat rows across the bottom of the cupboard.

Cracks in the wall fill up overnight and new paintwork covers them, so that in the morning there is no sign of the previous day's slide into disorder and decay.

The human body repairs itself. Wear and tear on body and brain disappears in the small hours of the morning. Cavities in teeth heal over, without benefit of fluoride.

Death when it comes is swift and silent, and at a time appropriate to the life cycle of the individual, but not a moment before, or a moment after.

So that there will be a general solution to the problem called 'the human condition' which will be arrived at from an analysis of the housework question and power in the family. Housework matters. It is a far from trivial issue.

The lunch table is cleared of food and the bottles are empty. The buzz of voices is pleasing, the sounds of people content for the moment with the pleasures of the day. I have provided well. The children flurry over the herbal tea. So many teabags, so many choices.

'Mother? Clara? What would you like? Some tea?' Mother holds out her arms. 'Butterflies,' she says.

Yes, it could be. Butterflies along her arms. 'Once I was covered in butterflies. The house, the garden that ran down all the way to the river. Before you were born. Hundreds of butterflies. Yellow, white, blue.'

Oh Clara, we bob at the edge of your awareness. It is a random thing, the death and destruction of the cells of the brain.

'Butterflies,' she remembers now. 'The black ones with the green and blue spots, like feathers. Down to the river they came, they settled on my arms, just like this. They drank from my arms – the perspiration, you see, sweat, they like it. They settle, and they drink right through the material, and their wings bob and shimmer and the green spots look like eyes. They push and they shove to get a space for their mouths. Butterflies, there, common as cabbage moths here. Rajah Brooke had one named for him, the birdwing. I saw it once, in the garden, near the river.'

Home sweet home.

Nobody leaves home any more.

The children don't leave home any more, nor do the grandchildren, nor the great-grandchildren. The first parents will ultimately leave feet first, after two hundred years or so, when they die, totally irreversibly, for the last time. The children and descendants stay on, for it is no trouble now the housework problem has received the ultimate technological fix.

Yes, one day there is an end to housework. Personal living tubes are set into the city walls in neat three deep layers. Each tube has its own self-shaking self-making bed, and all the in-tube life-maintenance and entertainment devices are superconductor charged and unbreakable. Electrostatic whizzers remove dust from all exposed surfaces within minutes of it settling and recycle it into the compost bin. Food still presents a problem, for though the quaint old-fashioned notion of a kitchen is gone for good, someone must still remember to recharge the Instamix and the Multiveg and the Compostacycle, and yes, you've guessed it, that still is women's work.

Things don't break down, any more, not exactly, now the entropy problem has been licked. It's more that things break out, sideways. Children grow rebellious and refuse to take their anti-entropy pills. Then they get cross and resentful when they find themselves prey to old-fashioned ills like acne and athlete's foot and influenza, the like of which was supposed to have been eradicated from all healthy human stock since the twenty-third century. Doctors then discovered that a thin layer of dust over things was positively health-promoting, so the electrostatic dusters had to be remodelled to allow for the retention of this much, and no more, of life-giving health-bestowing dirt. Although it seemed a good idea at the time to stick people in self-tidying tubes for twenty-four hours a day to stop them messing up the house, it was then discovered that people stuck in tubes all day grow tube-shaped in their body and tube-visioned in their mental outlook. Detubification reconditioning provided more work for psychologists than they could handle and so the doors of the tubes were swung wide for a few hours each day, to allow for what in the old days was called social interaction, or family feuds.

The back-to-the kitchen movement has started and the rot is beginning to set in. Soon there will come the breakdown of law and order as we know it, and the 'Back to the Trees' movement will herald the beginning of an irreversible decline into the squalor and degradation of the peoples of the twentieth century.

The Tea Room Tapes

In every department up and down the country there is a crisis. It's a scandal, and the cover-up is even worse. People don't want it known, their inability to run a tea club. Or else others might start to wonder at their ability to run the country.

It all started the day the tea lady didn't turn up with the morning tea. There have been some cutbacks, amalgamations and rationalisations round here lately. Or redundancies, sackings, lay-offs and push-outs. But when the tea lady goes, that's serious. Any one of us could be next.

No tea! No biscuits! Farewell to morning coffee! No warmth, no comfort! End of civilisation as we know it!

'No work!' said the juniors, mutinous.

'No pay,' said Mr Humphries, the boss.

'Oh, all right,' said the juniors, easily browbeaten, returning empty and forlorn to their keyboards.

The next stage was the

MEMO: Meeting.

SUBJECT: Tea crisis.

ATTENDANCE: One, the secretary Cathy, and she said she was only there to take the minutes. No one else came. They knew they'd be dobbed in to organise a roster, so they all stayed away. With the very best excuses.

So, there's nothing else for it but

ACTION: Ask Cathy to bring in milk each day on her way to work.

RESPONSE: No dice.

Dear Mr Blazer,
Re Terms and Conditions of Employment of Secretaries: Secretaries are no longer the lackeys of the bosses. They cannot and will not pop down to the corner shop on the whim of the management. Gee, Mr Blazer, sorry about this, but the boys in the union won't let me.
From
Cathy

SOLUTION: BYO milk.
CONSEQUENCE: Rampant individualism on milk front.
Four weeks later, forty quarter-litre cardboard milk cartons in the fridge, with green furry things sprouting from them and a smell that underlines what's rotten in yet another failure of departmental collective action.

Fridge a symbol of general decline of department under regime of cutbacks, lay-offs, sackings and redundancies. Entire department is composed of slime moulds and green furry things sprouting dusty antennae in vain attempt to keep ear well to ground whence rumours of cutbacks, lay-offs etc., spring.

HORNS OF DILEMMA: Sit there for week, until
DISASTER.

Young Philby makes his weekly report. He's dictated the forward planning policy statement for the next ten years, adjudicated the tenders for the satellite communications system, worked on the promotions criteria and selected the documents for shredding. If anyone needs milk in his tea, it's young Philby. I invite him to join me.

But it happened to me! My milk, my own small carton in the fridge, it's empty! And it was full only this morning.

'It's the milk bludger!' Cathy whispers to me. The milk bludger takes from the rich in milk and gives to the poor. It's a new form of crime in a department already riddled with every form of freeloading imaginable.

I don't want young Philby to know I can't organise a tea club. He isn't too happy with his cup of steaming milkless camomile tea, but he's learned not to ask too many questions. Can't stop him thinking, though I'm working on it.

This is the end. I must find the milk bludgers in our midst, and persuade them to see the error of their ways. Non-violently, of course. Cathy suggests a dye-bomb in the refrigerator. Must check if dye-bombs are in accord with department policy on apprehension of wrongdoers.

ACTION: Official caution placed on fridge.

Cathy does what she can. She takes a lurid red felt-tipped pen and writes a notice on the fridge. WE KNOW WHO YOU ARE and YOU HAVE BEEN OFFICIALLY WARNED and TAKE THIS AS AN ORDER TO MEND YOUR WICKED WAYS. CONSIDER YOUR COMRADES IN THE STRUGGLE, and so on.

CONSEQUENCE: Someone steals the red felt-tipped pen.

Then, one day,

SUCCESS! We catch the culprit! It's the janitor! It's Arthur!

CONFRONTATION: 'Arthur! How could you?'

BACK DOWN TO POSITION OF COMPROMISE: You'd think he'd just resign in shame. But no, not Arthur. He claims he has taken the milk with the very best intentions. He has taken from the bosses to give to the workers. He told the plumbers renovating the executive washroom to help themselves!

'You want the washroom finished?' asks Arthur. Of course I want the washroom finished! But not at any cost.

'Okay,' says Arthur, 'if that's the way you want it, just muck along without the executive washroom, see if I care!'

That will be taking things too far. As an executive myself, I stand to lose. 'Any other bright ideas?' I ask. Consultation, not confrontation, that's the name of the management game.

'I'll see what I can do,' Arthur promises.

ACTION: Janitor.

Ends in

RESOLUTION OF CONFLICT: Arthur comes good!

I am the first to congratulate him. We now have plenty of milk in the fridge! Arthur has seen to it. He makes us all pay something each week and is adept at extracting money from people who normally will not part with fifty cents for milk without protracted financial negotiations taking place over periods of months. 'Arthur,' I say with pride, 'you are obviously management material!' Arthur is pleased, but modest about his achievements. He does not give me the true story, nor do I press him. He has solved a crisis, and I am grateful.

Milk, milk, glorious milk! The sun shines every morning at ten thirty, the spirit is re-invigorated, the mind sharpened, the body is awash with liquid nourishment. Contentment reigns.

It doesn't last. It rarely does. Solve one problem, and it just raises others in its turn. Basic law of jungle and office life.

NEW PROBLEM: The invasion of the lollipop ladies!

Lollipop ladies! The women who help small children across the street on their way to and from school. Salt of the earth! Lovely people! I've nothing against them, but why have they invaded our tea room? Every time I go up there's a crowd of them going about their business. They come in a little after nine, when they knock off from duty at the school crossings, and they leave at three in time for the afternoon shift. They seem quite at home. They take off their white coats and their iridescent red-striped warning harnesses and they settle in for the day.

It's hard to pin down the moment it started. First there was one lollipop lady, then there were two, then the group just continued to grow until it took over the tea room. They bring their knitting and their lunch. Our tea room is warm. It has tables and comfortable chairs, and a nice view out over the trees. In spite of the invasion, it still seems to have plenty of milk for tea and coffee.

PLAN OF ACTION: Stand off and consider.

Did the boss order them in? I can't act till I find him and ask. Where is he?

Discover boss on conference leave and cannot be disturbed till the end of the duck-shooting season.

Oh. This calls for some

STRATEGIC INACTION: Sit on fence.

Pretend nothing has happened and that problem if ignored long enough will just go away.

SLIDE OFF FENCE AND FALL INTO CREEK: Bingo! They've started playing bingo!

It's not that I object to bingo on principle, but our part-time staff started to join in. Part of our response to the cutbacks, amalgamations, push-outs and shove-alongs has been to take on the part-timers, and we pay them next to nothing. It's no surprise to see them in there with the bingo, trying to upgrade their meagre paypacket to a living wage.

But I can't find a mention of bingo in the terms of reference for our department. Plenty of policy guidelines on everything else. No bingo, though.

'It's all right, love,' says Lurline, the leader of the lollipop ladies. 'Look at it this way. You start off doing one thing and business diversifies, see, in ways you never expect, and then, well, it's up to you to keep your eye on the main chance and get with the action. Go for it, Mr Blazer!'

Tell that to them in Canberra. They'll send in a Committee of Review and next thing I'll be working the children's crossing in a scarlet sash and a funny hat.

Lurline has an explanation. 'I'm here because I work here,' she says, 'and these are all my friends. There's Dot over there and Betty and Ron . . . '

'Funny, I don't remember . . . you work here?'

'Of course. Arthur gave me the job! He came down one day to the crossing and asked me to bring in the milk each day. He pays me a dollar a week. The money's not great, but it's no trouble: I enjoy it! And this tea room! It's so lovely! Warm and comfortable! And I can use it for my lunch, because I work here!'

At first nobody paid her any attention. We all thought she was one of the part-timers. They come, they starve for a while and then they go.

Of course for a part-time lollipop lady the lunch hour goes from nine to three. Hence the bingo. It all seems perfectly natural once it is explained to me, but I am uneasy. I search the terms and conditions of my employment. No mention of calling bingo anywhere.

It's all Arthur's fault! There he is, trying to slink past me on the other side of the corridor. I pounce on him. I no longer consider him potential management material.

'Arthur, what have you done?' I reproach him.

'I know, I know,' says Arthur.

'What am I going to do?'

'I didn't know about the SP bookies,' he begins. 'I swear I didn't!'

'What SP bookies?'

'They're not all members of the Mafia.' Arthur is on the defensive.

'What? The Mafia? Where?'

'The Mafia, they're the lot behind the roulette wheel.'

Roulette! The tea room is a casino!

Arthur shrugs his shoulders, and says he is sorry. Sorry! Ha! It's my fault. I should have remembered Arthur's genius for piling anarchy on chaos. For the moment I don't see how I can harness the Mafia to department-oriented ends. I'll just have to make sure the boss doesn't get to hear about it.

TOP SECRET: Casino facility.

'What's this I hear about a casino in your tea room?' asks the boss, the next time I see him.

'I forgot to mention it, Mr Humphries, sir,' I reply. 'On purpose. So you could claim you never heard of it, if it ever got out.'

'Good lad, Blazer,' says the boss. 'You'll go far.'

'Deniability, Mr Humphries, sir.'

'I've never heard of any casino,' says Mr Humphries. 'Who are you?'

I get back to Arthur. He has seen the error of his ways. He knows he should have been straight with me about sub-contracting the milk run to an outside operator. He should not have made the assumption that bringing in the milk was women's work, not now I've got the equal opportunity guidelines on my plate as well as everything else. I issue an official reprimand. 'Sorry! Sorry! That's not going to help when the next axe falls! Sorry isn't going to fix the roulette wheel! And if we all go, remember, we'll have to pay the full cost of all our paper clips and biros. For the terms of our natural lives!'

CRISIS MANAGEMENT: Dither indecisively while tea room enters rapid period of expansion. Events take on a life and logic of their own. Strategic inaction introduces laissez-faire economic system into tea-room accounting. Yesterday discovered three coalminers and a sky-diving team in full clobber, having tea and placing their bets on the outcome of the window-cleaning contract tender. Spa and sauna complex added to executive washroom. Computer dating service logs into the mainframe. Prize fights organised between automatic floor-washing machines. Helicopter landing pad requisitioned for roof, to bring in the tourists for the foreign exchange. Where will it end? I just sign the requisitions round here. No one ever tells me anything.

Take sauna and brood on problem of executive stress. Young Philby is beginning to suspect something.

TREACHERY: Philby dobs me into Committee of Review! They are coming to do us over!

ACTION STATIONS: Sit in a corner and chew handkerchief.

PROBLEM: Once we had no milk. We've solved that one, but in solving it we created a tea club which has taken off in highly irregular directions.

'What's this we hear about a tea club that has taken off in irregular directions?' asks the Committee of Review.

They want to examine the accounts!

'Accounts?' says Cathy. 'No accounts, as such. Plenty of tape recordings, though.'

Of course! The Tea-room Tapes! I should have known.

Potential for blackmail!

'Plenty of potential there?' ask the Committee of Review.

'In a manner of speaking,' I reply.

The casino is no longer a problem. Instead, it is the solution to all our problems! To the cuts! The lay-offs! The push-outs! The amalgamations! If we can add the attractions of the casino to the comforts of the tea room and take a percentage of the profits, then we've solved our funding problems. We're only doing what we've been told to do. We're hustling in the market place for our money and relieving the taxpayer of the burden. That's my job here, I see it now! To channel the talents and the skills of the whole department towards the private sector!

The Committee of Review are most impressed. 'Carry on,' they say, 'and have this award for initiative and sound management.'

Victory is relative, and I do not win all my battles. They promote young Philby for his percipience, and he sits in the executive sauna and simpers at me.

My secretary Cathy has left me for another department. She's left because of my inability to solve a milk crisis without blowing it up out of all proportion. Where she's gone they lock their milk in the fridge and they've given her the key. For the moment, Cathy likes it, but one day she'll find that power corrupts, and then she'll be back.

If You Go Down to the Park Today

A woman floats down the river, with flowers clasped in her hands. More flowers are twined through her long frizzy hair and they float out on the water in a becoming halo. She feels quite warm and rather drowsy, and for the moment is content to lie, eyes closed, and just let herself be carried along by the current.

Genevieve Howard is thirty-seven and might yesterday have thought herself too old for the floral frivolity in which she is now indulging. Today she is content to let it all happen. She is clothed in long flowing robes which swirl out around her, but they cause no trouble in the water. If anything they seem to buoy her up, not drag her down, which, on reflection, causes her some surprise. Then she realises how perfectly natural everything is.

She floats past a farm and neatly avoids, without even looking, two half-submerged tree trunks and a dead cow. It's as if someone up there was watching over her, and someone is.

Big Mother.

Genevieve floats on, soothed, supported and oblivious. She is surrounded by goodness and warmth. She has the delicious feeling that she could stop this delicious feeling at any moment, just by an act of free choice. She could feel angry, or sad; she could pull herself to the bank of the river and moor herself where the wild flowers and magic mushrooms grow down to the bullrushes on the shore, and give vent to wild crying or quiet exhilaration.

A thought starts to wriggle away in her mind. Wild flowers and magic mushrooms? How does she know? Her eyes aren't even open! She is amazed at herself. She has never seen a magic mushroom in her life! How does she know what they look like?

She opens her eyes and looks out on the world. Of course she's right! There are the mushrooms, looking just as they should! They are orange, with large white spots, and underneath each mushroom house sits a family of tiny elves! She smiles to herself and shuts her eyes again.

As she floats, European carp of enormous size and ugly complexion come up from below and nibble away at her toes. 'This will not do,' says Genevieve. 'This is just not good enough! I will not be nuzzled by a vile introduced exotic noxious European pest!' And the carp disappear and their place is taken by a shoal of tiny electric blue fish which skip and shimmer through the branches of purple staghorn coral. 'That's more like it,' she says. 'That's more what I expected.'

She drifts on into the city.

It's time for a change, and she decides she will get out and explore her new surroundings. Bells are ringing and bands are playing, and she feels good, until the feeling of being inappropriately dressed for the great occasion, of not looking entirely her best, comes over her. The feeling is triggered by the sight of her friend Helen, who is walking across to meet her. Helen Perry! Of course, Helen Perry would be here! She should have known. Helen is frowning though. She is dressed in the fashion of the city, while Genevieve is dressed in the fashion of the river. Genevieve realises she may well be overstated for the city, where a more formal elegance may reign.

Of course; thinks Genevieve, Helen never has approved of anything I wear!

Helen smiles, gives a quick kiss and is clearly keen to set Genevieve right. She shakes her head and, with a sorrowful smile, 'Oh dear!' says Helen, 'you people who come off the river, you're all the same! Just because you can wear long robes and flowing hair and flowers doesn't mean you have to!' Helen gives Genevieve a stern up and down look, taking in the plaited sandals and the lace fringe to the petticoat.

Genevieve says brightly, 'Helen! How nice to see you!'

Helen looks sternly at the flowers in Genevieve's hair. 'And what are those?'

'Um . . . primroses?'

'Come with me,' says Helen sternly.

'What's wrong with primroses?'

'Have you ever even seen a primrose?'

'It seemed like a good idea at the time,' Genevieve replies, reflecting that it is a good thing that she and Helen are very old friends, or otherwise she might take a vow never, ever, under any circumstances, ever to speak to Helen ever again.

'I see I shall have to take you in hand,' sighs Helen, in the infuriating manner of old friends who can be both rude and right. 'This looks more like it!' she says, as they enter the most elegant shop Genevieve has ever been in.

At first Genevieve is quite overwhelmed, but she soon finds she can cope with the people who flutter round her asking what Madam desires! As if she's to the manner born! Genevieve tries on clothes where mirrors show the perfect figure and the form divine (hers!), the cut elegant, the colour flattering. The first clothes she tries on are just right and she finds it absolutely incredible!

'It's absolutely incredible!' says Genevieve to the salesgirl.

'That's what they all say.' And the salesgirl smiles! Genevieve is stunned. 'Cash or credit?' she is asked. Genevieve has forgotten about the problem of payment. She's had no time to visit the bank, so she pulls out a credit card from her purse. But it is not the familiar green card she uses, vowing every time that it will be the last. No, it is a card she has never seen before in her life! White doves flutter from a hologram in the corner, swoop to the ground, pick up dollar bills and fly back to tiny shimmering trees to line their nests with money. The card is for Eternal Credit Unlimited!

'I really am awfully glad to see you, Genevieve!' says Helen, as they walk through streets paved with gold, with diamond-studded fire hydrants.

'Me too!' says Genevieve. 'I thought I wouldn't know anyone.'

'Of course, all this is for the tourists. This isn't the real city, not yet,' says Helen, fortunately before Genevieve can speak to indicate her very real pleasure at finding streets paved with gold, and diamond-studded fire hydrants.

Genevieve smooths back hair now neatly coiled in business elegance. 'I'll soon be starting a new job,' she confides. 'I'm going to be Peace, Participation and Equity Officer for the city.'

Helen is most impressed. 'So you got that job! Everyone was in for it! Congratulations! And you must have got it – on *merit* !'

Genevieve tries her best to look modest. 'I don't know about that
. . . well, perhaps . . . it isn't going to be easy, though.' Merit! Well,
perhaps Helen is right, thinks Genevieve. Merit is what other people
usually have, the people who get the jobs she doesn't get!

'I expect I'll see you around,' says Helen, as she drifts off into the
ether.

'Helen! Where do you live?' Genevieve calls after her.

'I'll catch up with you at the park,' calls Helen, from afar. 'That's
where everyone works.'

'The park? What park?' calls Genevieve.

'The Technology Park, of course.' And Helen is gone.

Of course, the park, says Genevieve to herself. She has travelled to
the great Technology Park in the sky, and the real work of her life is
just beginning.

A distant choir is at practice and the sun is setting in a rosy glow over
the river.

The arch over the street outside her room spells her name, in roses,
entwined. Genevieve is thrilled. 'Some merit,' she says to herself, as
she drifts off to sleep.

When Genevieve wakes in the morning, it is to a world where she
truly feels she belongs. She rises, and finds the roses in full bloom
across the archway outside her window. 'Some merit!' they say. The
sun is shining great beams of light through shimmering petals.

She sets out through the streets to find the offices of Peace, Participation and Equity Inc., who will be her employers. There's not a
park, as such, she begins to realise. The city is the park, and the park
is the city. Offices and factories are set in green fields with flowers
and walkways linking them together. She is walking while others
skate and glide and swoop and swing their way along. People nod and
smile as they pass.

Wait, though, if this place is truly perfect, why would they need
her? So there must be some room in which she can move, while all
around is pretty near perfect, but not quite. Proper perfection would
spoil the quest for others, and constitute a lack of perfection in itself.

The president explains Genevieve's job to her. 'The problem is that
everyone wants this life to be rather like the one they had before. Only

they want to feel more important. They all want to be king or queen. No one wants to wash the dishes or muck out the cesspits.'

Genevieve nods doubtfully. 'Cesspits?' she queries. 'Surely not here?'

'A primitive but brilliant touch,' says the president. 'It serves to keep us humble.'

'How extraordinary!'

'It serves to keep them humble. The people who muck out the cesspits.'

'It isn't at all what I expected from a Technology Park.'

'Of course we have the technology. But do we really need it? That is what the Technology Park is all about. Anti-technology!'

'Cesspits,' murmurs Genevieve. 'But I came to the park for peace, participation and equity!'

'Of course you did, dear,' soothes the president. 'Doesn't everyone?'

'Well, no! I thought it was *my* job! To make sure the park was run according to the principles of equity! And participation! And peace!'

'And so it will be, if that is what you want,' the president murmurs. 'All you'll have to do is to work out a way of satisfying everyone – kings, queens, sod-turners and secretaries – the lot. Participation! Yes, that's what participation is all about! Make them happy with their participation in the full range of human experience!'

'Even if they cop the rotten end?' queries Genevieve.

'Especially if they cop the rotten end! After all, someone has to dig the ditches and scrub the floors or the show won't go on.'

'I see,' murmurs Genevieve doubtfully.

'And someone has to float down the river, with rosemary and rue.'

How does the president know the manner of her arrival?

'Everyone has to get here somehow and you should see how some people drop in! You should hear the way some of them carry on! Complain, complain, about the arrangements! They don't want marble with those little pink flecks, they don't want to be too close to the railway line, they want a nice view, from the right side of the hill, facing the sunrise and preferably also the sunset. And no plastic flowers.'

'Let me get this straight,' says Genevieve. 'I have to give everyone an equal opportunity to do the washing up, and to muck out the cesspits, and to be king and queen and President . . . '

'No problems, are there?'

Genevieve smiles, with difficulty.

'Just let the free forces of the market determine the outcome! Those who can find better things to do, can go off to do them! That's what equal opportunity is all about! Equity! And those who can't find better things to do, well, they know that someone has to carry the spears and muck out the stables, or the play can't go on. So that's your job,' the president says to Genevieve. 'All fixed, all settled, all done. Any questions?'

'How? What? Where? Why?' asks Genevieve, as the president smiles gently at her and wafts off on the breeze.

'The first five years are the hardest!' The words drift back to her through the open window.

'What about peace?' Genevieve calls. 'You didn't mention where peace fits into this deal!'

'That's the easy part!' The words come back on the wind. 'To keep the peace, you have to prepare for war!'

'Wait!' calls Genevieve. 'That job isn't at all what I thought it would be!'

'Remember! Big Mother is watching over you!'

'Who is Big Mother?'

A light laugh echoes back from on high.

'How will I get to meet her?' calls Genevieve.

'Don't call her, she will call you!' The president is gone.

'I always think that someone has to carry the spears and someone has to put the rubbish tin out and someone has to muck out the cesspits, as long as it's somebody else.' Genevieve wheels around. She knows that voice! 'Lachlan! Lachlan McQuarie!' says Genevieve.

'I'm late,' says Lachlan. 'I got caught up at the flyover.'

Genevieve remembers those interminable union meetings, when she first got to know Lachlan. There he was, the bane of the bosses and the terror of the committee room, the person who made everyone else feel superior because without trying they had better manners, expressed themselves more succinctly and managed to sneeze delicately into their handkerchiefs, while Lachlan sat and spluttered and railed against everything and everyone. And furthermore, forced through his opinions by sheer force of attrition, while all seethed with irritation and boredom around him.

'What am I doing here?' asks Genevieve. She knows she can talk freely to Lachlan. Lachlan knows himself to be so much cleverer than anyone else that she need have no fear of making a fool of herself. Lachlan thinks her one already. So Genevieve can say what she feels. 'This job! Where do I start? It isn't quite what I thought it was going to be.'

Lachlan sighs. 'Nothing to it,' he says. 'Drop round to my place some time, and I'll fill you in on the scene.'

'Thanks a million,' says Genevieve gratefully. 'Once I get started, I think I'm going to like it here.'

'What, this dump?' says Lachlan, yawning, and looking out of the window as white doves flutter over trees laden with cherry blossom. 'Plenty of room for improvement.'

'Same old Lachlan,' says Genevieve, affectionately. 'I think the city's rather nice, just as it is. Though I'm not so sure about the park.'

'Same old Genevieve,' says Lachlan, as he prepares for take-off. 'Tap dancing on the Titanic.'

'Hey, Lachlan,' yells Genevieve, as he starts to follow the president out on the wings of the morning. 'When can I come to see you?'

'Any time!'

'Where?' Genevieve shouts anxiously. Lachlan is already far away.

'The Gene Factory!'

'Thanks!' says Genevieve, relieved. There's nothing quite like meeting an old friend who wants to set you right. And she has met two old friends! Lachlan and Helen! She now knows partly where she stands. The rest should be a breeze. Though what is Lachlan doing in the park? It's quite the last place she would have expected to find him.

What kind of technology is it in the park? If the president advocates the end of the septic tank, as we know it? It's true there is a 'Back to the Trees movement', hence the cesspits. Equally there is a 'Forward to the Stars' push, hence the need for peace, participation and equity. In short, some workers in some corners of the park regard other workers in other corners as too reactionary, or too revisionist, for their own good and the good of others. These then are the conditions of creative tension under which great ideas will flourish. They are also the conditions under which a lot of time is devoted to pointing out piously to others the errors of their ways.

It is a topic which Genevieve and Helen will discuss endlessly in the time to come. Genevieve will say that such a division of interests is lamentable and that everyone in the park should pull together towards their common goal.

'And what is that?' Helen will enquire.

'Why, perfection, of course,' replies Genevieve.

'Crap!' says Helen. 'We can't do that! We might arrive at the end!'

'At the end of what?'

'At the end of knowledge! At the state of perfect agreement! At the end of rational debate! At the end of the mud-slinging, the aspersion-casting and the state of feeling sorry for others because they know no better! Just imagine! What if it happened? Where would we both be?'

'Out of a job,' says Genevieve, thoughtfully.

'So, it's in all our interests that the park should continue as it is! That is why what we have in the park is right . . . it's a true democracy. Everyone works at what truly interests them. Everyone has their own version of the good life! Everyone is working towards that elusive common goal, perfection, if that's how you want to put it, but they are realising it, or not quite realising it because of the obtuseness of others, in various varieties of different ways. And the fact that they – we – are not quite realising it, why, that's the carrot on the end of the stick! That's why we all get out of bed in the morning!'

'Yes, but . . . ' says Genevieve. 'Does everyone have to pull against each other quite so much? All the time? In conflict and endless argument, in meetings which go on for ever and which decide nothing?'

'What did you expect?'

'I expected everything to be different. Not just the same only more so!'

'Better?'

'Yes!'

Discussions like this must go on for ever, without resolution, for coming to a conclusion upon which everyone will agree will end the game, and where will be the fun in that?

'Welcome to the Funny Farm!' says Lachlan McQuarie.

So this is what Lachlan is up to! Farming! Genevieve can't believe her eyes. Lachlan was always such a city boy, a hustler with one eye always on the main chance. They all thought he was up to no good with the union funds, though he did throw some great parties to which everyone came and wondered how he did it, while quaffing his champagne and scoffing down his oysters. 'However did you manage to get into the park?'

'Fast talking,' says Lachlan. 'You see before you the face of the future.'

Genevieve sees a herd of cows and a barn in the Technology Park. She remembers that Lachlan was sacked from his last job for insider trading and computer fraud. 'Are you in it for the money?' she asks.

'Who needs money where everyone has Eternal Credit?' Lachlan pats some bovine flanks. Genevieve keeps her distance. As far as she knows, cows have no part in her job to bring peace, participation and equity to the city. So she does not have to waste her time in making their acquaintance.

She's wrong, of course.

The cows are lovely, Genevieve has to agree. Big, too. In fact, huge. Larger than she remembered cows ever being, back in the old days. 'That's Bessy,' says Lachlan. 'We treated her with growth hormone factor back when she was an embryo, just whipped her out, did a spot of genetic manipulation and transfer, and just look at her now!'

'Hmm,' says Genevieve, 'and just what does that mean? Growth hormone factor, genetic manipulation and transfer? All that stuff?'

'Forty per cent more cow,' says Lachlan.

'So I see. She's huge!'

'Hence, it follows, 40 per cent more milk.'

'So, it follows, you need 40 per cent fewer cows?'

'Right on!'

'And 40 per cent fewer farmers?'

'That's the fatal flaw,' says Lachlan. 'The farmers don't like it.'

'What about the cow?'

'Look at it this way. She doesn't know any differently! Bessie doesn't know her mum was a midget and her dad was a bit of old leftover human growth hormone. She just gets on with life as she knows it, and doesn't she look just fine?'

'Won't you work yourself out of a job?'

'No, I won't be out of a job. Other people might be out of a job. But I'll still have a job. Putting other people out of a job.'

'I see,' says Genevieve. 'Is that right? Is it ethical?'

'Ethical? Of course it's ethical. If it wasn't ethical someone round here would have told me to stop doing it.'

'So you just do as you please until someone tells you to stop?'

'Doesn't everyone?'

'I don't know,' says Genevieve uncertainly. The cows, the lowing, the smell, the sun, the sound of the distant sea all combine to make her confused. She never knew she'd end up in a barn, when she took on this job.

'Wait, you haven't seen anything yet!'

Is Genevieve imagining it, or does Lachlan have a maniacal gleam in his eye?

'Behold,' says Lachlan, 'your brother the ass! Your sister, the cow! Meet Bessie, mark two!'

Genevieve sees a cow much like any other. 'What's wrong with the other cow? With Bessie, mark one?'

'What's wrong with the old model? I'll tell you. Too much milk!'

'But that was your idea! You made her produce it all!'

'Yes, but I wasn't to know, then, was I? I just went where the action was, and look! I'm copping all the flak! So I had to fix things up!'

'You didn't have to make them go wrong in the first place!'

'Okay, so we make more milk for other things! For instance, take Bessie mark two! Just an extra spot of genetic manipulation and embryo transfer, and Bessie two here produces human blood proteins in her milk!'

'Why?'

'It's simple once you think of it,' says Lachlan. 'It cuts out the middle man! Human blood from humans is full of all sorts of rubbish these days – AIDS, hepatitis and worse, if we knew the half of it. Now, take this cow here, no, not Bessie, take Flossie . . . actually, you can't take Flossie, I forgot, she's off having a spot of embryo manipulation and transfer at the moment.'

'So Flossie is going to be a mother?'

'In a manner of speaking, yes. Yes, she'll be a mother, but a very special kind of surrogate mother. Yes, Flossie makes a lovely receptive uterine environment, and no trouble with the lawsuits! We've fixed the cow to incubate the human baby. Cuts out the middle man! Or woman! Who needs the human womb any more? Childbirth, it's bloody and messy and inconvenient and a bore! We can do without any of that nonsense going on here! Now Flossie is the proud surrogate of both my kids, and there's nothing wrong with them! A spot of IVF, then into the cow and nine months later, the perfect baby! No bother, no trouble to anyone!'

'Lachlan!'

'And that's not all! Yes, the cow can then make human milk! No more night feeds at two a.m. and worse. No! The sky's the limit! There's nothing you can't do with science these days – and the child soon learns to hang on to mother! Human beings are so adaptable! Yes, my kids, they're both strong and healthy! They just love their roll in the hay and their salt-licks!'

'Lachlan! This is terrible!'

'Though they do have a tendency to moo at the full moon. Terrible? What's terrible about that?'

Genevieve will have to find Big Mother, quickly, and let her know what is going on!

'Of course it's what your job is all about. Participation! Equity! Participation in the full range of organic genetic experience! In the full range of possibilities in the entire animal kingdom! Not to mention also my brothers and sisters the plants, which we have not as yet managed to incorporate into the human organism, though we are trying, we are doing our best to overcome those obstacles an obdurate nature has placed in our way. No! We are no longer unfairly restricted to the genes we were born with. That was the real injustice, in the past. When Mother Nature used to get it wrong, far too often! When awful things happened all the time! What's so good about the old days? Let's toss out all the rubbish! Get the good genes working for us! Overtime! They don't complain, they're just lumps of protoplasmic goo! They lie there and take whatever we dish up to them. They're asking for it, let me tell you.'

'You may be right,' says Genevieve, faintly.

'We no longer have to strive for perfection! We can engineer it instead!'

'If you say so,' says Genevieve. 'Lachlan, why do it?'

'Glory!' says Lachlan. 'Credit! Being first! The ethic of conquest! Why not?'

Genevieve can't think of an answer, not right away. She resolves to go away and think her position through. She phones Helen. 'I need to speak to you. It's urgent! It's Lachlan! You know about his farm? He's not going back to nature! He's trying to improve on it! He's messing it around!' She explains what Lachlan is up to at the Funny Farm.

'But that's not right!' says Helen.

'Of course not!'

'It's hopelessly unethical! Has anybody asked the cow? Has Lachlan explained the whole process to her? I bet he hasn't! And has she given her consent, freely and in full knowledge of the aims and conditions of the experiment?'

'But Helen,' says Genevieve, 'that's not the point!'

'And the subject of the experiment has to sign a form! Green, A4, in triplicate! It's a good thing you came to me. I know all about ethics.'

'But that isn't what I meant at all! How can you get the consent of a cow?'

'Ask it,' says Helen.

'But cows don't have any moral opinions!'

'How do you know if you haven't made enquiries?'

'It's impossible!'

'Nothing is impossible! You never know until you try!'

'To get the consent of a cow?'

'It's your job! It's all about participation and equity.' Helen rings off in a huff. After all, Genevieve reminds herself, she got the job that Helen was after, so how could she expect total sweetness and light from a friend who is old enough to tell her where to get off? Indeed sour grapes now and then are perfectly understandable.

It was her job, but now Genevieve has quite made up her mind. If that's how Helen feels, then Helen can have it. Genevieve fluffs her hair around her head and arranges her lace petticoat so that a layer of it shows below her hem. She will take to the river again and find out what is around the next corner. She is big enough to admit she has failed, or shortly will be failing, even if she cannot properly be said to have failed before she has begun. If organising participation and equity is fraught with so many unanticipated problems, what about the problem of peace? She has not even started work on peace, indeed all she has to go on is the sinister remark made by the president at their last meeting: 'To keep the peace you have to prepare for war'. If talking to cows was part of her job, something which she considers has been unfairly concealed from her until now, then what else is there? What about peace, which she thought would be the easy one? Surely everyone wants peace. Don't they?

To prepare for war one must also prepare for war.

She has always thought that technology is good for you! And now she is beginning to wonder. Perhaps some of it is and some of it isn't. She has come to the great Technology Park in the sky and she has found it wanting. She does not know how she will ever begin to make sense of what is happening. How can she even begin to sort out a policy for perfection? She will only get it wrong and end up pleasing nobody. So she will cut her losses and run. It could be worse. What would happen if she stayed and tried to bluff her way through it? What if war were to break out, just as she started to sort out participation and equity? It would be an admission of her failure and a blot on her job résumé. So she will go, before it happens.

She will move on. She will go back into the river, and onwards to the next stop along the way. So she takes her robes and her petticoats, finds some flowers to twine in her tangled hair and feels all the better for it. Back to the river, and onwards, to the sea!

As she leaves, does she imagine it, or is that a choir of voices which is singing, 'Turn again Genevieve, turn back to the city. It is the city of light and love and joy'?

'And Lachlan,' Genevieve says. The voices fall silent. They know.

She slides back down into the water and sets off downstream. She feels relaxed and warm and nurtured. She soon finds out why. She is floating in the output pool of some kind of large electricity generating plant. There is a large red sign which reads 'Eternal Power Unlimited'. And there are large radiation warning signs! It is the effluent from a nuclear power plant! She has swung around to the other side of the city, and the warmth she has been feeling is thermal pollution! Some park, she thinks indignantly. In her next job she will put up a sign saying, 'Park. Positively no ball games. No Technology either'.

What is happening in the distance, outside the reactor building? It seems to be a demonstration! Genevieve moves forward and goes to see what is happening. 'At last,' she thinks, 'the anti-technology mob! And they are holding a demonstration! This is more like it!' She strides into the crowd, glowing with the joy of battle joined.

But what is happening? It seems to be a demonstration in favour of nuclear power! A celebration of the existence of the power plant! Genevieve cannot understand it! They are giving it a birthday party!

'Twenty-one years old today', one sign says. 'Still going strong on strontium', says another. 'Mummy's little baby, and who's a big boy now?'

Genevieve has never seen anything like it. 'What's it all for?' she asks the people holding placards. The men are wearing three-piece suits and the women colour-co-ordinated golfing gear.

'Nuclear power for a better world!' they tell her.

'It cuts down on the acid rain.'

'Helps prevent the melting of the polar ice-caps.'

'It fills a vital ecological function.'

'And what is that?' asks Genevieve.

'It keeps us warm in winter.'

'But so can alternative sources of power and energy!' says Genevieve. 'What's so great about a nuclear reactor?'

'No rubbish! No smoke! No dust!'

'No rubbish? What about the plutonium?'

'That's easy! It recycles plutonium!'

'It's very conservation minded.'

'What about the high level nuclear waste?'

'It's used for bombs! Nuclear warheads! Multiple anti-personnel dispersal units!'

'This is terrible! I can't agree with all this!'

'What, you want us to dump our plutonium on some unsuspecting rubbish tip?'

'No! Why bombs?' asks Genevieve. 'What do you want bombs for?'

'To kill people.'

'Whatever for?'

'Before they kill us.'

'We're past all that now!'

'Don't believe it for a moment. You know that lot down there on the other side of the park, in the Gene Factory?'

'I've heard of them,' says Genevieve savagely.

'You've got to watch out for them!'

'I know!'

'They tell you they're only making bigger cows, but we know better! What are they doing with twenty tons of anthrax spores and half a test-tube of genetically engineered rattlesnake venom?'

'Twenty tons of anthrax spores and half a test-tube of genetically engineered rattlesnake venom? They didn't show me that!'

'They wouldn't, would they?'

'I always knew Lachlan was a rat!' says Genevieve. 'He must be stopped!' The president said that to keep the peace you have to prepare for war. Perhaps other people are right and she has been wrong in believing in peace and love and ecologically sound means of energy production. Though 'Two wrongs don't make a right,' she says.

'Nor do two rights make a wrong!'

'I don't understand.'

'We are right to recycle our plutonium. It's the socially responsible and politically aware thing to do! Now, over on the other side of the park, they think they are right in going in for biological warfare. What else can they do with twenty tons of anthrax spores, once they've got them? Both sides are right!'

'Hang on a minute,' says Genevieve, but the crowd is going wild now that three robots have appeared on the top of the stairs. They are waving regally at the crowd.

'Give her a kiss Charlie!' they yell.

Two of the robots embrace, and the crowd screams and shouts with delight and bursts into a lively chorus of 'Why were they born so beautiful?'

'What about the fallout and the increased cancer rate?' asks Genevieve when the uproar dies down.

'We have a responsibility to future generations.'

'What?'

'Don't you see? Radiation is essential to introduce change and variation into the system.'

'To cause mutation!'

'Why?'

'We don't want to stagnate in a biological backwater!'

'No, we're a true democracy here! We give the genes a greater sense of participation in the life of the city!'

'What if change turns out to be for the worse?'

'What is worse? What is better? It's all relative!'

There is no arguing with them, but Genevieve is determined not to sell out the ideals of her youth. So she can't just give up her job, as she was planning. She will have to see it through to the end.

She is beginning to work out what is happening. At first, she was delighted with all she saw in the city. It seemed to her to be perfection. But as she learns more and moves about the place, she is discovering that she is intruding into other people's ideas of perfection. So, is she right and are they wrong?

Something within Genevieve says 'Yes!'

Should others be allowed to go their own way within the park, so that the various different and competing views get equal shares? Fair turns? Or should she seek to impose her views of perfection on others?

'Yes!' says Genevieve.

'Why?'

'Because I am right and they are wrong!'

'How do you know?' asks a small still voice.

'Because I am Peace, Participation and Equity Officer for the city! I am not the War Office! I am not the Nuclear Regulatory Body! I am not the Biological Hazards Committee! I am the person charged with peace! Participation! And equity! It is my responsibility! War is totally out of the question!'

'Turn again, turn again Genevieve,' the voices sang to her on the river, and perhaps they were telling her to go back to the river and back to the city. She lets herself sink into the waters. But they sweep her outwards to the sea! Of course, she should have known! It is one thing to float down a river, but quite another to float back up it again.

'I don't care,' she says. 'I can't solve their problems for them. Nobody will ever listen to me. I might as well spend the rest of my life on a desert island.' But she knows it's the wrong thing to do. It would be a dereliction of duty and a blot on her job record to give up now. She will have to return to the city and do her best.

How?

'Big Mother, I need you now!' cries Genevieve. And Big Mother is listening! Big Mother hears her. Big Mother comes to her rescue! Only it takes Genevieve a time to work out what is happening.

At first it seems as if she has reached dry land of some kind. She finds she can stand up, though she hears no sign of waves crashing on a beach, nor can she see any sign of palm trees. But her feet are on a slippery surface and soon she finds she is rising up above the waters! On the back of a whale!

'You called, my child?' a voice asks, from the deep.

'Big Mother, I need your help! Where are you?'

'You're sitting on me!'

'I seem to be sitting on a whale,' says Genevieve. 'That's why I need your help! Get me off!'

There is the sound of jolly rumbling and deep laughter. 'That's me!'

'Oh. Pleased to meet you,' says Genevieve. 'I'm sorry, nobody told me your species.'

'Nobody thinks that kind of thing is very important, over in the city. They tend to forget that it means a great deal where you've just come from.' The whale is a very big whale indeed and Genevieve is glad that all she can see is a wide expanse of black back with a blow-hole at the top.

'That must be it,' says Genevieve. Though she could kick Lachlan and Helen and the president for forgetting to mention that Big Mother was not quite human in form. Of course, now she thinks about it, there is no reason why she should be.

Now Genevieve has found Big Mother, she will not let her go without telling her the terrible things which are going on in the city. Messing about with genes! Deliberately breaking down the species barriers! Nuclear bombs! And biological warfare! There is so much that she doesn't know where to start.

'I was hoping you'd drop by,' says Big Mother. 'I know you've been so busy since you arrived, but there's so much to learn! I'm so pleased with the city and what they are all trying to do there! The cows that give birth to babies, the bacteria that are liberated to new ways of life, the way the whole biological world is sharing and parti-cipating each in the other! What do you think?'

'Aaark,' squawks Genevieve. 'Of course, I haven't had time to get adjusted to all these new ideas yet.'

'Of course! I quite understand,' says Big Mother.

'I don't think much of the bombs.' Genevieve is determined to make some kind of protest.

'Oh, neither do I, dear, but what can you do about them?'

'Tell them to stop it!'

'Stop it! The simple direct approach! What a clever idea! I'm so glad you've come to join us!'

'But you'll have to tell them to stop it! They won't listen to me!'

'I can't interfere in the running of my creation. It's supposed to be a participatory democracy of the most advanced kind.'

'That's the problem,' says Genevieve. 'They'll put everything to the democratic vote and nothing will ever get done!'

'Ask the president for help.'

'The president isn't any use! It's hopeless! I need power in order to win this one! Real power!'

'I wish I knew what I could do to help,' says Big Mother. 'I'll just take you in to land and drop you off over there by that cathedral for my worship.'

'You can help me, you can!' Genevieve slides down off the whale's back and into the shallows. She swims round so she can look Big Mother in the eye.

'Tell me, how can I help? I really must dash.'

Genevieve takes a deep breath. 'Make me empress! Empress of the Joyous City! I'll need real power, not just the illusion of power, if I am to sort out all their problems.'

'But who will do your job? Peace, Participation and Equity Officer? It's so important!'

'Give that job to Helen! She wanted it in the first place.'

'Why ever not?' says Big Mother agreeably.

'Remember,' says Genevieve, 'I'll be needing power!'

'And you shall have it!' says Big Mother, preparing to dive. 'You shall be Empress of the Joyous City. You have got the job on *merit*. Give it a year and see what you can do.' She departs with the wind and waves.

Genevieve goes forward, into a new world.

Tremendous Potential for Tourism

Ancient seas have washed this place. Layers of sandstone have been laid down, consolidated, then as the waters fell, exposed to the power of wind and rain and fire and flood. The earth moved uncounted cycles round the sun, and lakes formed and filled then shrank and dried and turned to salt, leaving fossil relics of the death of early life. Once, twice the ice came close, but never quite this far. Ice could not tame this southern land, and it fell back before the forward march of sand-dunes and stony plains. It rained more then, ten thousand years ago, and the lakes held fish. Crabs scurried on the mud-flats, and the reedbeds sheltered wildfowl. But the rains were never certain, and grew scarcer as the ice-caps shrank, the plains rose from the sea and the desert thrust forward with dunes and drifting clay.

These were slow changes and they passed unnoticed then, by people who learned to live in their new lands. First grass grew scarcer, then died out completely, and they must grind the small chenopod seeds for flour. Fresh water retreated below the surface of the rivers, and they must dig down deep for it. Change came, and with change came adaptation to the change, and the people lived with the new conditions and survived the harsh changes to their lands.

Some live there still.

The tour-guide explains

Here we are at Burrakana, a name meaning 'place of rainbow waters'. Yeah, I know, where are the Rainbow Waters? Place names round these parts are pretty ancient and the rainbow waters were round here somewhere. Before the last Ice Age or something.

Some words of caution before we go in. All dust-raising activities should be avoided. That's what they tell us. Pretty difficult I know when all around is dust, dirt and desert sand far as the eye can see. Basically what it boils down to is this. Don't sneeze when you stand on a historic site.

We'll stop here at the forward gate for fifteen minutes. Down there's the old Army dunnies, ladies to the left, gents out the back. The original blew off in the last blast, but they've cobbled it together again in roughly the same location. With a pile of old newspapers on a rusty nail. For the authentic experience.

Yes, Mrs Isuzi, I am afraid that is the full extent of the ablutions block. No flush facilities this side of the Emu Hilton.

You have fifteen minutes exactly.

From the Official Tourist Guide: some features of general interest

The historic site of Burrakana is situated on Tietkens Plain north of the Nullabor and south of the Great Victoria Desert. The word 'desert' may initially mislead, but once travellers have seen the mallee gums and the bull-oaks, the mulga and the salt-bush, they know deep down the desert thrives after its own fashion. Burrakana is a bird-fancier's delight, with parrots, hawks, and wedge-tailed eagles. There is an occasional camel, though the visitor should note that the camel is an introduced species and not a native inhabitant of the area.

Kangaroos hop among the quandong trees, the shy bush-turkey peeps out from the bright red blossom of the Sturt Desert Pea, lizards sun themselves among the spinifex, rabbits have adapted the numerous historic concrete slabs as cool roofs to their burrows.

* * Definitely worth a visit.

A scientist gives an interview

Rabbits, bloody rabbits. That's the good thing to come out of Burrakana. Didn't kill them off completely, except the ones we hit at ground zero, that's how we chose the sites to explode the bombs, got to have some reason for doing things, the biggest burrows in the territory, don't say we're all cold and uncaring, deep down we care, we really care, about the rabbit problem.

Didn't get them all the first time, but we kept trying, 756 experiments later, I can claim, we shortened the lives of the surviving rabbits well and truly by half. That is a great victory in the ceaseless and unremitting war against the rabbit which Australia has been waging ever since some idiot let a couple loose in the bush two hundred years ago.

Turns out the buggers love the concrete slabs! The ones we poured over all the contaminated equipment! They like a cool roof over their head, so they search out the concrete and burrow like crazy underneath! Why didn't we line the pits with concrete, put in a bottom and some sides, you ask me, but I can tell you now we did it on purpose to get the bunnies! There's always a reason for something when you get right down to it. They get into where the plutonium is thickest and it half-kills them off. Shortens their life by half, and the half-life of a rabbit means 50 per cent fewer rabbits, stands to reason.

Tracking the buggers after they come out of their radioactive burrows coated with a fine coating of plutonium dust is a problem. Have you ever tried to collar a rabbit? So there is no evidence that the rabbits spread the plutonium around, because we never really ever got round to looking for whether they did or not. Nobody gave it a thought at the time. So here is absolutely definite scientific proof that radioactive rabbits pose no adverse health risk whatsoever.

The half-life of a rabbit, that's how we measure radiation these days. How much plutonium does it take to shorten a rabbit's life by half? Instead of mentioning emotive terms like radioactivity, we now put it in terms of so many half-rabbits, and it doesn't frighten the children.

That's the story of my involvement. I don't know anything about anything else. No black mist. No dead people. Just rabbits.

The tour-guide's spiel, continued

Here at Burrakana we're not like other tourist towns. We actively encourage scavenging! We throw souvenirs in free! A lump of metal here, a piece of rusty wire there, a bit of fluffy yellow uranium oxide, some pellets of cobalt-60, or a piece of glazed fused sand, old cables, brass canisters – they may seem small things, insignificant in themselves, but they all add up. So feel free to help yourself to as many bits and pieces as you like. That way we'll soon export it all back to where it came from, or near enough. Anywhere in the northern hemisphere will do.

See those old sheds? The world's one and only plutonium mine. Yep! Look at it this way. Plutonium is a feature of the man-made landscape here at Burrakana. They don't have it too many other places. It was one of those things that happened, something nobody really noticed at the time, but later! Later it takes off and blows up and there's trouble for you.

So we fixed it all right. Dusted the plutonium off the bunnies, sifted it out of the sand, melted it off the wrecks, wiped it off our feet after the rain. Sticky stuff, gets into everything, and if you should happen to find yourself out in the rain and stuck to some plutonium dust, remember – stand still and try your best not to breathe until help arrives. Just one or two particles, inhaled, give you a 50 per cent chance of lung cancer. Heads you get it, tails you don't.

What did they do with all the waste? Well, that's a bit of hush hush, but rumour has it that it all got shipped back to London and dumped in the Thames. Ha, ha, only joking, Mr Templeton-Thwaites.

From the Official Tourist Guide: some features of archaeological significance

Architectural interest is added to the Burrakana site by a plethora of decorative concrete plinths. Tastefully truncated small white pyramids commemorate the sites of important experiments. Here the tourist will see history in the making, for the plinths are the pyramids of the future. The pyramids of Egypt have stood 6,000 years, but that is nothing compared to the pyramids of Australia, which must mark this site as dangerous for one million years approximately. The pyramids of Burrakana will stand until they crumble, spelling out the following important message:

166 *The Total Devotion Machine*

WARNING. RADIATION HAZARD. RADIATION LEVELS FOR A FEW HUNDRED METRES AROUND THIS POINT MAY BE ABOVE THOSE CONSIDERED SAFE FOR PERMANENT OCCUPATION.

It is acknowledged that there well may be a hieroglyph problem in half a million years. Hence the radiation logo is deeply though tastefully engraved into the plinth, a Rosetta Stone for the benefit of far future visitors, extraterrestrial or otherwise.

It is considered likely that the plutonium will outlast the message.

Other architectural features include the Tietkens Plain and Bula Cemeteries. Plain smooth concrete slabs mark large burial pits. Visitors often comment on the absence of the usual inscriptions to the dead. It is because these cemeteries are different. They contain radioactive waste of various kinds, though nobody knows quite what is buried where. Nobody knows quite where the people killed in the tests are buried either. It is assumed that the sky is their canopy, the desert sand their winding sheet, the birds and spinifex their companions. It is noted that they would have preferred it this way.

A scientist gives evidence

Q. People reported a black mist which drifted across their lands and made them sick.

A. We have consulted our documents and we know, categorically, there was no black mist.

Q. Then why do they talk about it?

A. These people tell each other stories. Stories are anecdotal evidence. Our evidence is scientific. The black mist never happened. And if it did it must have been something else. A rain cloud. A mirage. A figment of the imagination. A collective hallucination. Mass hysteria. That kind of thing. It happens all the time.

Look where the stalk of the mushroom cloud rises to the sky. Dust to dust, red dust to black dust, dry dust to sticky dust, plain dust to radio-active dust, blue sky to firestorm, sweet rain to poisonous fallout. The dark mist of the earth brings death. They know it in their bones. Their radiant bones.

Q. Are the tests dangerous?

A. Many people have been genuinely worried about the alleged danger to health caused by our nuclear tests in Australia. This anxiety is completely unfounded. There is no risk. Trust me. I know. You don't.

Black mist of the earth, the transformer, the bringer of death.

A. But we didn't know anyone was there!

Q. Did you look?

A. They told us the land was uninhabited, a wasteland.

Q. Did you look?

A. We did not see.

The tour-guide's spiel, concluded

Hey, you at the back of the bus, can you hear me? As you leave, throw your badges into this bucket here. Any old how. Just like in the old days. It adds the element of authenticity.

It's all over now, those times. The bombs, the tests, the radiation. Just a passing phase.

Now we've got lasers in space, we don't need the dirty bombs. We've got nice clean ones up there, instead.

Cut me, I bleed, beat me, my bones break, cast me out into the wilderness, and my mind grows mad. Bomb me, I suffer, starve me, my body is covered with sores. Torture me, I break, I scream, I suffer in terror, I die.

I am not alone. The earth has millions like me.

Pollution is an ephemeral thing, from the point of view of the rocks. In the future, some sediment will be discovered, a layer marking the ancient place of the rainbow waters. There it will be, fossilised and radioactive. Travellers will come to this planet and they will marvel at a band of rock which is different from the rest. They will talk about us as once we talked about the dinosaurs. 'Their brains were too small for their huge bodies,' they will say, nodding wisely to each other.

One day we shall be food for alien thought.